WITCH'S WRATH

WITCH'S WRATH

THE NOMAD WITCH™
BOOK EIGHT

TR CAMERON   MARTHA CARR   MICHAEL ANDERLE

DISRUPTIVE IMAGINATION

DON'T MISS OUR NEW RELEASES

Join the LMBPN email list to be notified of new releases and special promotions (which happen often) by following this link:

http://lmbpn.com/email/

This book is a work of fiction. All of the characters, organizations, and events portrayed in this novel are either products of the author's imagination or are used fictitiously. Sometimes both.

Copyright © 2024 LMBPN Publishing
Cover by Fantasy Book Design
Cover copyright © LMBPN Publishing
A Michael Anderle Production

LMBPN Publishing supports the right to free expression and the value of copyright. The purpose of copyright is to encourage writers and artists to produce the creative works that enrich our culture.

The distribution of this book without permission is a theft of the author's intellectual property. If you would like permission to use material from the book (other than for review purposes), please contact support@lmbpn.com. Thank you for your support of the author's rights.

LMBPN Publishing
2375 E. Tropicana Avenue, Suite 8-305
Las Vegas, Nevada 89119 USA

Version 1.00, September 2024
ebook ISBN: 979-8-88878-690-1
Print ISBN: 979-8-88878-492-1

The Oriceran Universe (and what happens within / characters / situations / worlds) are Copyright (c) 2017-24 by Martha Carr and LMBPN Publishing.

THE WITCH'S WRATH TEAM

Thanks to our JIT Readers:

Christopher Gilliard
Diane L. Smith
Dorothy Lloyd
Dave Hicks
Zacc Pelter
Jan Hunnicutt

Editor
SkyFyre Editing Team

DEDICATION

For those who seek wonder around every corner and in each turning page. Thank you choosing to share the adventure with me. And, as always, for Dylan and Laurel, my reasons for existing.

— *TR Cameron*

CHAPTER ONE

Scarlett Prynne blinked as she stepped out into the sunlight in Austin, Texas. She hadn't realized they'd spent so much time lingering over breakfast. At her side, her magical companion Runeclaw also blinked as his eyes narrowed in response to the brilliant morning. She complained, "Almost headache-inducing."

He replied, "Not as much as being back at this hotel."

"Oh, please. It was fine."

"Just had to come back in search of ghosts, didn't you? Couldn't resist one more try."

Scarlett shrugged as she slipped a hand into an inner pocket of her leather jacket to grab her sunglasses. "We had a free day."

He swatted her leg with a paw. "And we wasted it here instead of doing something fun, useful, or both."

"I admit it is unfortunate that we didn't see any ghosts, not even the ones we saw before, but I wouldn't call it a waste."

"Clearly you and I have different definitions of both 'unfortunate' and 'waste.'"

Scarlett slipped on the sunglasses and looked around. Her motorcycle, Dusk Runner, was parked a dozen feet away. It gleamed in chrome and black, its surface covered in arcane symbols that Maddox, the leader of the Spell Riders, had etched for her. The bike's magical defenses were still active, and it appeared they had been sufficient to keep anyone from bothering her precious vehicle.

She frowned as a pair of men in leather jackets on motorcycles turned their heads toward her as they rode by. The expression deepened at the sight of a man standing at the corner in mirrored sunglasses. His head had turned in her direction as well. She activated the communication earpiece nestled invisibly in her ear. "Amber, are you there?"

The Witches on Wheels' infomancer replied after a second, "Almost. Just bringing a cup of coffee back to my computer. What do you need?"

Scarlett pictured the woman sitting in front of her computer rig at the warehouse with a fond smile. She and Amber had become friends during the adventures they'd shared. "Some people around here look a little off. Can you run some facial recognition for me?"

"Of course." A window appeared in Scarlett's glasses, which were much higher tech than they appeared, and an array of images flashed by as the man she'd seen was tested against pictures in the database. It took only a handful of seconds for a match to appear. Amber said, "Ex-military, honorable discharge, now working for a defense contractor."

Scarlett asked, "A legitimate one?"

"Doubtful. Look around the area some more." As Scarlett complied, the infomancer grabbed pictures of people's faces and repeated the scan through the database. "Another. And another. Mercenaries, I'm thinking."

Runeclaw muttered, "Just had to come back, didn't you?"

Scarlett replied, "Maybe it's unrelated to us."

The cat countered, "If you believe that, you're more of an idiot than I already think you are."

Scarlett walked toward Dusk Runner. "One way to find out for sure."

Amber asked, "What's that?"

"Capture one and have a chat with him." Before she'd taken more than a few steps, men identical in body type and wearing serious expressions below their mirrored sunglasses stepped onto the main street from an alley and moved toward her with intent. Scarlett reached into her sleeve for her wand and cast a veil to conceal her and Runeclaw. Now invisible, they raced for Dusk Runner.

Amber used the remote piloting module to start the bike's engine before Scarlett reached it. She climbed on, created the force band for Runeclaw to latch onto, switched on the bike's active protective enchantments, and gunned the engine. She bounced up onto the curb, and even though she was invisible, the mercenaries sensed the danger in time to jump out of the way before she could run into them. She revved the engine, swerved back onto the street, and sped off.

A moment later, Amber said, "You've got pursuit."

"How many?"

"I see four motorcycles plus some cars. I can't be sure yet if the cars are following you or just a coincidence."

Scarlett grinned and increased her speed. She loved riding. "Let's find out."

She raced for the nearest edge of town, scanning the area ahead to ensure no enemies were closing in from that direction. Runeclaw asked, "Why is it we're not portaling again?"

"I told you. We need to have a chat with one of these guys."

"You might have noticed that they outnumber us rather substantially."

Scarlett laughed. "When has that ever stopped either of us? And don't try to be the voice of reason, cat who jumped through an enemy's portal without knowing where it went."

Runeclaw sniffed. "That was a calculated risk."

"So is this." Dusk Runner shot through a light just before it turned red, and Scarlett heard screeching and horns behind her as the pursuers blasted through the intersection.

Amber said, "All right. We've got four motorcycles more or less together. A Jeep and a pickup truck right behind them. Another Jeep and pickup trailing a little behind. There might be more. It's pretty active around where you are at the moment."

"The more the merrier. It'll give Runeclaw something to do, which might stop his whining."

When they blasted across the town limits onto a road with dirt and shrubbery on both sides, Amber said, "Keep it steady for a minute." As Scarlett obeyed, the small box mounted to the side of her motorcycle in front of one of her saddlebags opened. A moment later, the whir of turbo fans sounded as the small drone buzzed out of its container and into the air. The box closed automatically. Amber said, "All right. Cameras are active. I don't see any sign of an ambush ahead, so the only identified threat is those trailing you. I think we might have a second wave behind the first, though. Probably bad guys who weren't close enough to the vehicles to react immediately."

Scarlett asked, "How are they arranged?"

"Jeep on the left, pickup on the right, the four motorcycles in two ranks between them. Definitely a couple more vehicles close behind. I make it to be one Jeep and one pickup."

"How many people?"

"I only see drivers. But they could be concealing passengers with magic, and the pickup trucks could potentially have heavy weaponry in them."

Scarlett's grin was devilish. "They don't realize I've got heavy weaponry too and that they've bitten off way more than they can chew."

Runeclaw asked, "Are you sure we need to talk to one of these guys?"

"Positive. Come on, where's your sense of adventure?"

"I left it behind at the Driskill Hotel with the antisocial ghosts."

"Wimp." Scarlett swerved the bike to avoid a vulture that inexplicably landed in front of her motorcycle and muttered, "It's a good thing I don't believe in omens."

Amber said, "Unless you speed up, first group will be

with you in thirty seconds. Second group will arrive about three minutes after that."

"Plenty of time."

"Anything you need from me?"

"Go back in time and put an armed drone on the bike instead of a surveillance one."

Amber laughed. "A drone that size would only have BBs to shoot."

"Fine. If you're not going to fulfill my very reasonable request, then make sure the landing pad in the warehouse is ready for some captives."

Runeclaw replied, "Captives, plural? I thought we just needed to have a chat with one."

Scarlett bared her teeth in a grin filled with the energy that came with impending combat. "Well, if the first one doesn't want to talk, we'll have a backup."

"Why not just take them all?"

"Don't tempt me, cat."

Amber warned, "They're ten seconds behind you. They'll be in firing range shortly."

Scarlett rolled her neck. "Then let's get this party started."

CHAPTER TWO

Scarlett checked her rearview mirrors to verify her trailing enemies' positioning, then hit the button to deploy what Maddox had called his favorite weapon. She swerved left, then diagonally to the right as the bike plowed forward. Behind her, sharpened triangles of metal called caltrops spilled out onto the road. They were virtually invisible in normal circumstances, but she caught a glint from the sunlight as she looked back. It wasn't enough to save those trailing her, however.

The first two motorcycles struck the caltrops without any attempt to evade. The front wheels exploded, followed a moment later by the back ones. Motorcycles and riders transformed from rolling objects to ones that slid along the pavement with occasional flips and flops. Scarlett hoped the riders were wearing appropriate armor under their clothes.

The truck and the Jeep pulled off to the sides, and both remaining motorcycles went to the right to avoid the caltrops. Scarlett curved to the left, figuring she'd deal with the solo enemy first. The truck's driver had controlled the initial slide from hitting the dirt, righted himself, and was now plowing forward. She raced toward him, lifted her wand, and sent a fireball careening across the gap between them. He saw it coming and wrenched the wheel to the side. The truck almost went over, two tires on the same side lifting before the driver yanked the wheel again and got all four tires on the ground.

Scarlett bit off a curse and pulled her wheel sharply to the right as gunfire sounded. She snarled, "He does have a passenger, and the passenger has a gun." She rode in a serpentine as she gained some distance, then curved back around. She snarled another epithet at the sight of the Jeep that had joined the pickup truck. "How much time before the rest get here?"

"Approximately two and a half minutes."

"Plenty of time," she murmured as if to convince herself it was true. Scarlett raced toward the pair, intending to pass beside one of them so they blocked shots from the other. Automatic rifle fire came in at her from that direction as whoever was shooting traversed their weapon horizontally, and she snarled and moved into the middle of the two vehicles. Another stream of bullets from the other side kept her in place. It was clear they intended either to ram her when she was between them or to shoot her while she was without any other defenses.

Runeclaw asked, "Is this a good idea?"

Scarlett replied, "They don't know who they're fooling with." She waved her wand and created a force ramp in front of the motorcycle. It was a technique she'd used before, and it worked as well this time as it had previously. By the time she crossed paths with the other vehicles, she was too high for those inside to get a shot. The bike landed hard, and it took her several seconds to bring it back under control and spin it around in the opposite direction.

Runeclaw observed, "You're a crazy person."

"Crazy like a fox. Get behind me."

Runeclaw didn't argue. He jumped to her shoulder and down her back. She created another force band for him to hold onto. The enemy truck and Jeep were in front of her, and the distance was closing fast. This time, they tried shooting her directly instead of trying to be fancy. She swerved the motorcycle left and right, then barked in pain as a bullet caught her arm. The level of burning told her it was only a graze, so she ignored it and raced forward, leaning down to make herself a smaller target.

At the last minute, she wrenched her wheel to the right to put herself on the outside of the pickup truck. When she was abreast, she hit the toggle to fire the needle guns on that side. Maddox had installed the launchers and guaranteed that anything beside her when she used them wouldn't be there for long. As usual, he was correct. The long metal slivers shot out, blew the tires, pierced the metal, and struck the driver. The pickup truck swerved and struck the Jeep, then tumbled behind her as she brought the bike around again.

Before the Jeep could regain control, she launched a fireball at it. The magical attack hit squarely on the rear panel where the gas cap was, and a moment later, the car exploded. Scarlett wrenched her bike into a curve and headed toward the road. She cast a veil again, then slowed to avoid wiping out as she crossed the pavement to the other side. Amber warned, "Two more motorcycles, plus a car and Jeep over there, too."

"Time to try out our other toy, then." Scarlett pushed a button on the handlebars. The motorcycle interfaced with her display glasses and showed her two crosshairs, one red and one blue. "Red." She used the tiny joystick on the handlebars to move the crosshairs over the pickup truck. "Lock." The crosshairs moved with the truck. "Blue." She repeated the process with the car. She angled Dusk Runner to make both shots as equidistant as possible, then pulled the trigger.

A decorative element on the front of her motorcycle disintegrated as two rockets shot out of it. They trailed smoke as they hurtled through the air, making them visible to her enemies. The targets reacted immediately, changing direction to evade them, but it was no use. She and Amber had decided on fire-and-forget missiles, and these used thermal sensors and pattern recognition to maintain their lock. Her targets had no chance of escaping.

She searched for the motorcycles and spotted them stopped a distance away. The missiles hit almost simultaneously, and the two larger vehicles burst into pieces as they detonated.

Scarlett used the distraction of the fireballs they created to change her position and approach the motorcycles from the side. When she neared them, they were already in motion toward her previous location.

Amber warned, "One minute, maybe less before the rest of the party gets here."

"Not a problem."

The motorcyclists were shooting pistols one-handed, and while several buzzed close enough to sound like oversized bees, they didn't get closer, even though they were using anti-magic ammunition that would pass through her shields like the earlier shot that had gotten her arm.

She lifted her wand as she reached a range that would mitigate their reaction time and sent a blast of force magic out of its tip. It crossed the distance to one of the motorcycles in an instant and blasted the rider off.

As the other one flashed by, a sizzle from behind told her Runeclaw had attacked as well. She twisted, saw the electricity covering the rider on the other bike, and watched as his hands left the handlebars. The motorcycle's front wheel hit something and dug in, propelling the rider through the air as the bike tumbled behind him. Scarlett used force magic to catch the flying figure and lower him to the ground. She grabbed the one closer to her with force magic, lifted him, and carried him behind her as she rode toward the other.

She parked Dusk Runner, dismounted, and dropped him. A wave of her wand opened a portal. The people she'd requested were on the other side waiting for her. She floated the first man through, then the second.

Amber advised, "I've got the bike. Go."

The sound of rumbling engines from the road was all the incentive she needed.

Scarlett stepped through the portal with Runeclaw at her side and closed it when they were through. She saw the feed from Amber's drone in her display glasses as the infomancer piloted Dusk Runner away.

"I'll bring it back to the edge of town and conceal it somewhere so you can get it later."

Scarlett replied, "You've still got the needle guns on the right side if you need them."

"Noted. But I'm not nearly as much of a trouble seeker as you are."

Runeclaw, who heard the comm chatter over a small speaker on his collar, laughed. "And there's the truth of it. Trouble is attracted to Scarlett like a bee is attracted to pollen."

Scarlett shook her head at him. "Maybe they were after you."

"You're suggesting they brought trucks and guns to get a cat."

"You are pretty wily."

Lin, the drow who was her best friend among the Witches on Wheels, sauntered up. "No, this one's squarely on you, sister."

Runeclaw said, "I told her going back to the hotel was stupid."

Lin shook her head with a look of remorse. "She just never learns."

Scarlett pinched the bridge of her nose. "Shut up. Shut up, shut up, shut up. No more from either of you."

One of the Witches who'd been standing around gestured at the two captives they'd just handcuffed and ankle manacled. "What do you want us to do with these?"

Scarlett grinned. "Take them into separate interrogation rooms. I'm going to get cleaned up, and we are all going to have a chat. If they're good, maybe they get out unscathed. If they're not, Runeclaw gets to use them as a clawing post."

The cat replied, "I like the sound of that. Let's just do that instead."

"No, we have to give them a chance to help us first."

"Lame."

CHAPTER THREE

After returning to her hotel to shower and change into a pair of comfortable jeans and a black T-shirt, Scarlett and Runeclaw returned to the warehouse. Lin sat in a chair in front of the area set aside for prisoners and nodded at her approach. "Got them both in here ready for you. One of them is way more annoying than the other. What's the plan?"

Runeclaw replied, "Good cop, bad cat."

Both women laughed. Scarlett said, "Maybe not. Let's try being nice first and see what that gets us."

Lin raised an eyebrow. "Feeling optimistic today, are we?"

"One can hope, right?"

Runeclaw countered, "If one is stupid, I suppose."

The drow rose from her chair. "Left or right?"

Scarlett replied, "Left."

Runeclaw countered, "Right."

Lin shook her head. "I'm going with the cat's answer. His claws are scarier than yours." Runeclaw offered Scarlett a haughty glance as he trotted toward the room in question. Scarlett shook her head, looked up to the ceiling, said a small prayer beseeching the universe to grant her patience, and headed in after them.

The off-white room was about ten feet by ten with a concrete floor and a single chair bolted into place beneath a stark light fixture. A man was secured to that chair with his arms behind his back. He had a long, dirty beard, a wrinkled face with pock marks on one cheek, and wore a sneer that showed yellowing teeth in addition to his motorcycle jacket, jeans, T-shirt, and boots. "Well, well, well, if it isn't the witch herself." His voice was gravelly.

Scarlett responded with an overly enthusiastic smile, "So wonderful to be appreciated."

"Let me out of this chair, and I'll show you some appreciation." He smacked his lips. "Mmm-hmm."

Lin stepped forward and delivered an open-handed slap to the side of his head. "Behave, scumbag."

He grinned at her. "Never have, never will."

Scarlett asked, "What's your name?"

"Witch killer."

She rolled her eyes. "I see we've got a clever one here."

Runeclaw suggested, "How about a little lightning to motivate him?"

Scarlett grinned at her partner. "We don't need to electrocute him just yet. But if he continues to be a jerk, maybe I'll let you offer him some encouragement to change his attitude." When she turned her attention back to the man, he looked a touch worried but hadn't lost his bravado. "All right, if you don't want to give me a name, how about you tell me what your motorcycle club is called?"

"It's called 'Bite Me.'"

Lin barked a short laugh. "Wow. This guy's a real treasure. All the snappy comebacks."

Scarlett pinched the bridge of her nose and suppressed a sigh. "Okay, then how about we cut to the chase since you're not interested in being civilized. Who hired you?"

The man grinned. "Somebody who's gonna find you, beat you down, and kill you after they cut on you for a while. Shame I won't be there to watch, but maybe they'll video it for me."

Scarlett opened her mouth to snarl a response, but a lightning bolt shot out of Runeclaw's tail and wreathed the man in forks of electricity. He shuddered under the sustained barrage until Scarlett snapped, "Runeclaw." After a few extra heartbeats, the attack fell off.

Lin stepped forward and put two fingers on the unconscious man's neck while she looked down at his chest. "He's still breathing, and his heart's still beating. You stopped the cat too soon."

Scarlett shook her head at each of them in turn. "You're both feeling rather nasty today, aren't you?"

Runeclaw replied, "He deserved it."

Lin confirmed, "He absolutely did."

Scarlett said, "Let's try not to incapacitate the one in the other room until we get some information, okay? Can we all agree on that as a starting point?"

Lin gave a theatrical scowl. "I suppose."

As Scarlett opened the door, Runeclaw replied, "No promises."

The second room was identical to the first, but the man

inside it was not. He was younger, free of facial hair, and visibly nervous.

Scarlett sat cross-legged in front of him, far enough away that he couldn't reach her but near enough that she could speak in a normal tone. She wondered how long it had been since he'd made the jump from probie to full member if he had done so yet. "What's your name?"

"Lyle."

"Nice to meet you, Lyle. I'm Scarlett."

He nodded. "All right."

She leaned forward. "Can you tell me a bit about your motorcycle club? I'm a member of one myself, the Witches on Wheels."

Lyle swallowed as he nodded again. "We don't have a name officially. Our symbol is the skeleton. We generally refer to ourselves as Bones."

"Like all of you individual bones put together make up the skeleton?"

His quick smile was sharp as if it hurt him to do it. "Yes." She sensed that he was working hard not to shake from the stress of the situation.

Lin turned away and whispered toward the corner, doubtless sending that information to someone. Scarlett replied, "Good. Thank you. So, why were you all after me?"

He didn't answer at first. His gaze traveled the room, looking at her, Lin, and Runeclaw, whose tail emitted a quick spark under the man's gaze. He swallowed again. "We were hired."

"By whom?"

"I don't know. I'm a newer member of the group. They don't tell me much."

Scarlett nodded. "Anything you can tell me would be good."

Lyle looked down at Runeclaw again. "I overheard someone saying it was a wizard and a man in a suit. I don't know anything else. They gave us your picture and the cat's picture. Although, really, there aren't many people who wander around with cats, you know? Not exactly low profile, traveling with a cat. I mean, we didn't need the picture. Of him."

Scarlett let him babble for a moment longer. "What were your orders?"

His already pale face lost more color. "To capture you, if possible."

"And if that wasn't possible?"

"To kill you. And the cat."

She nodded with a smile that said he'd only told her what she'd already known. "Have you done that before?"

He tilted his head. "Killed a cat?"

Scarlett closed her eyes, begged the universe again for patience, then opened them. "Killed anyone."

Lyle shook his head. "The group, yes. Me, no."

Scarlett didn't think they'd get anything more out of him but repeated the questions to be sure. His responses didn't change. Finally, she asked, "What would you do if we let you go?"

He stammered, "I'd run. You'd never see me again. The group would never see me again. I'd be gone."

Runeclaw let out a cough like he had a hairball in his throat. "He's lying. And he's bad at it."

Scarlett nodded. "I agree. That's not true. So, we'll call Diana and store him with the others."

Lin said, "I'll take care of that. You two can go rest or whatever. You've had a long day, and it's not even midafternoon yet."

Scarlett didn't feel like resting, so she and Runeclaw headed for the metal stairs that led to the second-floor office. Inside, Amber sat bathed in the glow of her screens, which provided the only light in the room. Black plastic covered the window that would have looked down over the warehouse.

Amber asked, "You both okay?"

Runeclaw leapt onto her desk and nuzzled her hand in reply. Scarlett said, "Yeah, we're fine. How's Dusk Runner?"

"Waiting for you in a rented garage near the hotel, fully shielded." Scarlett let out a breath as the infomancer dispatched her worry about her beloved motorcycle. "The drone recapture didn't work right, so you'll need to go get it when you retrieve the bike."

Scarlett grabbed the room's other chair and pulled it next to Amber's. "Have you been able to track down what this was all about?"

Amber gestured at the screens. "Traffic cameras, store cameras, I've got all the surveillance. They had people all over town in Austin. Only a portion of them managed to join in the chase."

Scarlett shook her head. "I wonder how they knew I'd be back there."

Runeclaw interjected, "They gambled on you being stupid. Evidence suggests that's a pretty safe bet, wouldn't you say?"

Scarlett stuck her tongue out at the cat as Amber replied, "Oh, they've been watching other places too."

Amber called up other images, and Scarlett recognized them as the streets of Provo, Utah.

She asked, "My friends there?"

Amber replied, "All warned, all safe."

A sudden thought occurred to her. "Are the Spell Riders in danger?"

The infomancer laughed. "Only an idiot would take them on. That garage of theirs is a fortress of magic and weapons."

"Really?"

"Really. They hide it well, but it's there."

Another worry dispatched. "I'll need to visit them to get Dusk Runner ready again."

Amber brushed a stray hair out of her face. "Probably better to wait until tomorrow. The bad guys might be watching for you to come back."

Scarlett looked over at Runeclaw. "We could spend the day and night at the Driskill. See if we can spot any more ghosts."

He growled, "I'll murder you, and you'll be one of the ghosts."

Amber laughed.

Scarlett joined in as she replied, "Okay, not that, then."

The cat offered a condescending nod. "Wise choice."

CHAPTER FOUR

Camus sat behind his desk in his comfortable chair and made notes with his favorite fountain pen in the journal he used for everyday thoughts. Each glide of the nib on the thick paper was a pleasure, bestowing a feeling of accomplishment, of progress. He kept his deeper plans, magical records, and other vital writings in his basement sanctuary, where he used an even more pleasurable fountain pen and special, magical, long-lasting inks.

On one side of the page before him were listed the names of the people he'd invited to the gathering and a summary of what he knew about them. On the opposite side, he'd written the names of the collared servants he sought to place, along with notes about their looks and abilities.

His task now was to find the best way to match those in the left column to those in the right. He also needed to keep an eye on what would be necessary to convince the powerful people to accept one of the servants he was offering them. They all had the money to afford it and the status to hide the purchase. That wasn't the issue. But matching personalities from one column to the other was a mental challenge, and taking concrete steps toward the Veil's ultimate goal was always a pleasant way to pass the time.

It was also a way to make the waiting less painful. He'd received word earlier that the witch had been spotted but had received no update. He hadn't insisted on one, figuring Ellis would bring him the important information as soon as it was available. Nevertheless, the open-endedness was an ongoing distraction. A knock on his door caused him to close the ledger and slip the pen back into its holder. "Come in."

Ellis entered, wearing his usual dark suit and open-necked white shirt with his carefully styled hair all in place. He didn't look as happy as he might have, however, which lent a sense of foreboding to the moment. Camus asked, "You have a report?"

The other man nodded. "Yes. The men pursued the witch as she rode off on her motorcycle."

He interrupted, "She didn't just portal away?"

"No, sir. She led them out of town, then attacked."

"The result?"

Ellis straightened as if steeling himself. "She killed several of the men pursuing her and captured two of them."

Camus grinned. "And?"

Ellis nodded with a grin. "The trackers are working exactly as we anticipated they would. We have their location."

Camus leaned back and laughed at the good news.

"Excellent. It's always fun to turn the tables, isn't it?" After one of their former captives had been tracked with a medical implant and rescued by the witch, Camus had arranged a delivery of those implants. He'd had them injected in all the people they'd hired to watch for the witch against the possibility of this exact thing happening. The mercenaries had been dubious, but a bonus payment had quashed their concerns. While it would have been far better if one of those people had put a bullet in the witch's head, this was still progress of a sort.

Ellis asked, "How would you like to handle it?"

"Check the place out as best you can, but under no circumstances allow the effort to be detected, even if it means we don't get as clear a picture of their operation as we'd like. They'll doubtless have guards and sensors and such, and we can't allow them to know they're being watched. Surprise is everything."

"Of course. When do you want to move on them?"

Camus considered the question. "Too early, and they might have time to regroup. Too late, and the attack might get in the way of the gathering. So. Four or five days before the gathering."

Ellis frowned. "That doesn't give us much time to prepare."

"It can't be helped. That's when it will be least dangerous to our plans."

"Magical support?" He was asking if Camus or the remaining Robe would attend.

Camus shook his head. "Hire some. I'll not risk myself or Gold." A flicker of nervousness crossed Ellis' face. "What?"

"Are you concerned that the Veil is down to only you two, now?"

Camus tugged his sleeves out of his jacket, one after the other. "Not at all. This was always the goal, although having my other loyal subordinate killed was unfortunate. We will rebuild."

"Family heirs?"

"Where it seems appropriate."

"And where it doesn't?"

Camus leaned forward and picked up his fountain pen. "We'll kill off any members of their families who know about the Veil, then find new members from more dependable families."

Ellis understood that Camus wasn't interested in further pursuing that line of questioning. "Did you want to use the same mercenaries?"

"How did they perform?"

"About as well as can be expected."

"Then yes. I trust your judgment on this."

Ellis nodded. "Very good." He left the office.

Later that afternoon, after the close of business, one of the wizards on the security team portaled Ellis to the mercenaries' headquarters building. The defense contractor that was the top-level company had its fingers in all kinds of pies, although they didn't generally admit to the clandestine mercenary unit he hired. Knowledge of them was primarily spread by word of mouth among those who needed to hire such people.

The secretary at the desk welcomed him and unlocked the elevator. A few moments later, he was up in the corner office. The nameplate outside the door said Flynn Johannsen, but Ellis doubted that was the man's real name. The room's occupant rose, shook his hand, sat, and gestured him to a chair. "What can I do for you?"

Ellis lowered himself into the chair. "We failed to get the witch today."

Flynn shrugged. "I warned you mixing bikers in might be a bad idea."

Ellis lifted a hand. "You were probably right, but in any case, I'm not here for blame games. Because of the miss, we'll need the full package."

The man's grin showed his teeth. "Tactical situation?"

"Attack on their facility. Likely one or two large buildings. Possibly a tavern."

The man lifted his cell phone from the desktop and typed in a few things. "Defenses?"

"Unknown, but they'll definitely have magical protection."

He tapped the phone again. "Objective?"

Ellis replied, "Kill or capture everyone inside, then destroy the place or places."

Flynn looked up and scratched his chiseled jaw. "We could hit them all with rockets. Simultaneous attack. No warning."

Ellis had thought of that already and eliminated it as an option. "They might have more than magical defenses, and their magic might also be able to deal with the rockets. We've only got one shot to surprise them, so it'll have to be down and dirty."

Flynn lifted an eyebrow. "Full package indeed, then. That will cost you."

"Understood, and not an issue."

A grin blossomed on the other man's face. "That's why I like working with you. Prep time?"

Ellis winced internally. "Only a few days."

Flynn gave a sharp nod. "Additional fees."

"Of course. Half now, half later?"

Flynn shook his head. "For an op like this, all in advance. We'll have some outlays and will have to pay for speed in hard currency."

Ellis frowned. "I can do that electronically, but not in cash like usual."

Flynn rose and extended his hand as Ellis did the same. "Fine. We can get it converted. My infomancer will talk to yours."

"Pleasure doing business with you." Ellis navigated down to the lobby. Then his wizard portaled him back to Camus' estate house. He immediately headed for the security area and found the woman in charge of security for the gathering. He asked, "You've heard?"

She nodded. "Yeah. That woman is slippery."

"That's one word for it. Lucky as hell, too."

"What are we going to do about it?"

He grinned. "The backup plan worked. We have a location on them."

She clapped her hands together. "We're going to kick their teeth in?"

He shook his head. "The mercenaries I just hired are going to kick their teeth in. *We* are going to stay focused on the gathering. But I want you to do something extra."

She nodded. "Everything is running smoothly. We'll have visible people, hidden people, the whole nine yards. I've got the bandwidth to take on something else."

"Make escape plans for Camus and Gold. I want three different plans for my review for each of them."

"They go together?"

He shook his head. "No. Make Gold more visible. If we can get him away, great. If he distracts anyone who thinks about crashing the party, that's a greater benefit as well. It could help save Camus."

She stared for a second. "Does the boss know you're doing this?"

"No. And we're not going to tell him. He's got enough to worry about."

"Do you really think there's a danger?"

He sighed and ran his fingers through his hair. "No, but I would've said the same thing about the collaring ceremony and the crafting session before that. The witch and her friends have a tendency to show up when you don't expect them. So, we need Plans B through Z to deal with them."

She gave a decisive nod. "You've got it. Count on me."

He pinned her with his most serious look. "I am. Be worthy of my trust."

CHAPTER FIVE

Early the next morning, Scarlett and Runeclaw portaled to just outside the Driskill Hotel. After looking around carefully and seeing no watchers, they walked to the garage that Amber had used to secure Dusk Runner and called the infomancer.

A loud groan was the first response, then Amber asked, "What?"

"We're at the garage."

Amber yawned loudly. "Why are you even up yet? Why is anyone?"

"Not all of us stay up until the wee hours of the morning."

"You should have respect for those who do." A moment later, the garage door rolled up. "There. Now let me go back to sleep."

Scarlett laughed. "We still need to know where the drone is."

"I hate everything and everyone. Go west, like the band said. I'll talk to you when you're close."

Scarlett rolled the bike backward out of the garage and climbed aboard. She summoned the force band for Runeclaw, and he jumped up in front of her and dug his claws into it. She asked, "Good?"

Her partner replied, "Great day for a ride."

"Couldn't agree more." Scarlett searched the streets for any sign of surveillance as they rode out of town. She saw a few people she thought might be watchers, but she spotted no pursuit in her mirrors, and Amber didn't warn her of any. After they crossed the boundary that demarcated the area claimed by the town and were on the highway, Amber announced, "All right. Here's your beacon."

A small pulsing dot appeared in Scarlett's glasses, and a moment later, a small map with a colored line showed her the path to take. "Got it."

"I set it down in a bunch of shrubs, so it might not be visible right away."

"Good deal. Go back to bed."

The infomancer laughed. "Oh no, now I'm up, and I'm mad. If anyone asks why, I'm gonna tell them it's your fault. Also, watch out for snakes. I bet there are snakes there. Snakes that specifically want to bite you."

Scarlett snorted. "Awesome. Thanks."

"You deserve it."

"Harsh, but possibly true." After a few more minutes of riding, Scarlett came upon the site of the battle with her pursuers. Pieces of cars still littered the area, although the largest bits had been taken away.

She rode on, guided by her map, then pulled the bike off the road and bumped over rocks and dirt until she reached a small patch of shrubbery. The drone was nestled inside it. She climbed off and removed it, hit the button to open the box on the side of her bike, and placed the drone inside. A small green light began to blink to indicate it was charging. "Well, at least that part works."

She climbed back on. "Off to see the Spell Riders, I guess."

Runeclaw replied, "It's kind of early. Maybe we should ride around for a while."

Scarlett grinned. "Now that's an idea I can get behind." She pulled the bike back onto the road and headed in the same direction, away from the rising sun. After an hour of admiring the scenery and enjoying the freedom of the road, she reluctantly pulled the bike over, climbed off, and cast a portal to the Spell Riders' garage.

She pushed the bike through and discovered the garage was not at its normal activity level this early in the day. Maddox and Snow sat in lawn chairs outside the corner, so she parked her bike and headed over.

Snow raised his coffee cup as if in a salute. Scarlett replied, "Same to you. Coffee?"

Maddox leaned over, grabbed a thermos on the ground next to him, and tossed it to her. She unscrewed the lid and poured the life-giving liquid into the cup with the thermos. Maddox began, "Look what the cat—" but got no further.

Runeclaw interrupted, "If you say it, I will claw you within an inch of your life. The scars will be horrifying. Children will run. Women will weep."

Snow and Maddox laughed, then Maddox mimed zipping his lips shut. Snow frowned. "Look at all the scuffs and scrapes on Dusk Runner." He shook his head dramatically. "I told you not to entrust such a wonderful motorcycle to someone as kooky as Scarlett."

Maddox rubbed the back of his neck with a sigh. "It's true. I think what you actually said was that she's a wildcard who would probably hurt herself and the motorcycle."

Snow winced, then admitted, "Yeah, that sounds like me. It doesn't appear as if I was wrong."

Scarlett said, "Damaged in a worthy cause. But if anyone should be blamed, it's Runeclaw."

The cat growled, "Lying liar."

Maddox stood with a groan and stretched. "Wheel her over to my area. Let's take a look."

Scarlett complied, with Runeclaw riding primly on the bike, and soon was watching Maddox at work. The mechanic worked with a simplicity and economy of movement that was always pleasant to watch. He reached into a nearby toolbox and pulled out six needle pods. The cylindrical disks held the needles under compression to a third of their size, made possible by a clever articulated design. They snapped out to full extension as they launched.

He asked, "How did they work out?"

"Perfectly. Just like you said they would. Killed a truck with ease."

He grunted in satisfaction, then busied himself removing the empty pods and installing the new ones. When he finished that, he asked, "What kind of missiles do you want? Fire-and-forget again?"

Scarlett nodded. "Definitely. Being able to launch them and know they'll get the job done while I do other things is perfect."

He detached the remaining pieces from the first

launchers, then mounted a duplicate on the bike. She had to agree that it looked odd and messed with the motorcycle's streamlined look, but it wasn't an obvious telltale of weaponry inside. Finally, he went to the back. "The caltrops storage is empty. How did they work?"

She grinned. "Perfectly."

He laughed. "They always do."

"Unfortunately, the drone didn't."

Maddox finished reloading the caltrops and closed the container, then lifted the drone out of its container. "Doesn't look damaged. What's the problem?"

"It didn't return to the bike. The remote-control module worked great, though, by the way."

He turned the drone this way and that, then shrugged. "I'll have to get with Amber to see if it's a hardware or software issue. Meantime, let's take care of some of these scars." He brought out buffing cloths and a motorized polisher and went to work on the bike. It didn't take long for him to clean up most of the visible blemishes. One of them crossed an enchanted glyph. He pointed at it. "We'll have to redo that."

He placed the tip of his wand on the damaged area and spoke a few words. The metal smoothed out as if the glyph had never been there. Then he brought out his engraving kit. "You can do this one." He handed her the vibrating tool she'd watched him use to put the markings on the motorcycle.

"All right, how?"

He cast another spell and glowing lines appeared on the bike. "Trace that with the tool. While you do it, you need to push your magic into the symbol, focusing on it just as you would to create a shield but not actually creating it."

It took Scarlett several tries to get the magic right, but with his guidance, she eventually managed to store the spell in the glyph. When she gave it a pulse of magic to activate it, the force shields snapped into place perfectly. He grinned. "Good work."

Runeclaw observed, "And you didn't blow us up while doing it. Pleasant surprise."

Scarlett replied, "You're such a supportive presence."

"I do my best."

Snow interrupted them. "If you're done with the bike, I'd like to steal Scarlett."

Scarlett looked at Maddox, who nodded. She rose and followed the Spell Riders' artificer back to the small room at the rear of the garage that he used as a magic workspace. Inside was his ritual ring, which was active, protecting a small box set in the center. He deactivated the ring and stepped inside. She joined him, and he reactivated the magical protection, opened the box, and took out the collar she'd found in an abandoned rail workshop. He turned it this way and that, seeming as amazed as he always was at the craftsmanship. "I've been working with the collar in my spare time. It's an impressive piece of work."

Her eyebrows rose. "Oh?"

Snow nodded. "Yes. As evil as it is amazing, of course, but still impressive. What I didn't realize before is that they're all linked."

Scarlett blinked in surprise. "What?"

"Yep. It turns out that shielding it in here was a very good idea. Although I'm not sure the creators realize they're linked." His tone said he was thinking deep thoughts about magic and technology.

"You're not making sense."

Snow laughed. "A common occurrence, I'm afraid. It's a trait of the magical metals. They're all somehow part of a whole, and all things made of them are connected somehow. It might be connected to the unprocessed ore, too, but I'm not positive about that."

Excitement sparked inside Scarlett. "So, you can locate the other collars?"

"Not yet, unfortunately. Discovering the connection is only the first step of a long journey toward the destination of actually using it. But I'll keep walking that road and see where it leads."

"You're the best."

He grinned and twitched his wand to spin the collar in the air like a coin ready to reveal heads or tails. "I know."

After they'd put the item back in the box, she returned to Maddox, who displayed the cleaned-up motorcycle. "You know, we've got bigger bikes here we can customize for you."

Scarlett put her hands on the handlebars. "Shh. She'll hear you. I'd never give up Dusk Runner."

Maddox laughed. "That's the right answer."

Scarlett wheeled the bike and its feline rider out. "Catch you later, magic man."

He called, "Keep her out of trouble, Runeclaw."

The cat snorted. "As if such a thing is possible."

CHAPTER SIX

Scarlett spent the afternoon on menial but essential tasks like washing clothes, mending gear, and sharpening blades. Her chores took longer than expected, and she didn't make it to Wheels until about eight o'clock that night.

She and Runeclaw walked in to discover the place was as boisterous, loud, and laughter-filled as before the mess with the Veil had started. She spotted Wren at a table, walked over, and sat in close talking distance. Runeclaw jumped on the table. The leader of the Witches on Wheels grinned. "Not bad, huh?"

Scarlett replied, "Busy. Really busy. Is that a good idea, given all the things and stuff?"

The other woman shrugged. "We need to keep that income flowing. We've got contracted security around the perimeter to watch over the place."

Scarlett looked around and noticed that many of the Witches on Wheels were present, more than she remembered being there back when she'd first encountered the club. "Offering up a target too tempting for the Veil to resist?"

The corner of Wren's mouth quirked up. "No. Just making a buck. But if it accomplishes both things, I wouldn't be unhappy."

"The Witches are armed?"

Wren nodded. "And indulging lightly."

Scarlett's next question was interrupted as someone called for Wren from the far side of the room. Scarlett headed to the bar and bumped fists with Lin, who was bartending. The drow slid a bottle of beer to Scarlett, and she noted it was one with a comparatively low alcohol content. When Lin returned from waiting on a couple of other customers, Scarlett commented, "You would think the Veil would be tempted by this."

Lin nodded. "The shotgun under the bar is loaded."

"I can't imagine they'd be stupid enough to come after us here again. What do you think their endgame is?" Ever since Snow had brought the collars back to the forefront of her mind, Scarlett's brain had been chewing on that question.

"Control, apparently."

"But of who? College students?"

Lin ran a bar mop over a ring of condensation. "Maybe they're practice. A dry run. Making sure the magic and technology work."

Scarlett drummed her fingers on the bar. "Seems a long way to go for that, though."

Lin reached under the bar, extracted an open bottle of root beer, and tilted it to her lips. She returned it. "Yeah, I don't get it either."

"Maybe they're just evil?"

Runeclaw, who had jumped up to sit on the bar, observed, "Evil usually has a purpose, no matter how misguided. Unless the perpetrators are insane, I guess, but I don't think that's the case here. They seem too organized to be crazy."

Scarlett replied, "Well, what could that purpose possibly be?"

A new voice joined the conversation as Amber slid into the stool beside Scarlett. "I don't know the answer to that question yet, but I might have a way to find out."

Scarlett twisted in her seat to face the infomancer as Lin leaned closer and asked, "How?"

"I've dug up another company that Kingston Trane has a connection to."

Scarlett asked, "What kind?"

"Robotics."

Her mind immediately snapped back to the robots they'd fought at the extraction site. "Interesting."

Amber nodded. "Right? Anyway, maybe there's something there."

Lin handed the infomancer a bottle of soda. "So why don't you sound excited?"

Amber frowned. "If I breach their system and I'm detected, that's two data points that connect to Trane."

Scarlett replied, "Who is our only lead at the moment. He hasn't moved?"

"No, just hanging out at his house still. And the trace will only work for a handful more days."

Wren joined them. "What's up?" Amber explained, and

Wren remarked, "Fortune favors the bold and all that. I'm always going to default to action."

Lin replied, "Sounds right to me. Action gets my vote."

After Scarlett and Runeclaw agreed, Amber conceded, "All right, I'll do it."

Scarlett asked, "When?"

"No time like the present."

Thirty minutes later, Scarlett and Runeclaw were in the warehouse office, seated behind Amber as she typed on her keyboards. Scarlett asked, "Do you think you'll be able to avoid getting identified?"

"I'm definitely going to do my best to be a ghost. I'm routing everything through extra proxies. It will slow my signal and hamper my abilities a little, but it's worth the anonymity. Should give me a little more time to break the connection if I'm detected, too."

"Is there any way to make it look like we're after someone other than Trane?"

"Good thought." Images flicked by on the screen, faces, websites, streams of information. Finally, the infomancer continued, "I can deploy some searches for other members of the organization, ones that would be easier to discover than my main effort. That should at least give them a false lead to follow."

Runeclaw asked, "Won't they know it's fake since it's less well hidden than your other efforts?"

Amber shrugged. "Maybe? Not sure. That's a discussion that will become a circle really fast. I think we'll have to hope for the best."

Scarlett asked, "Before you jump in, is everything okay in Provo?"

Amber snapped her fingers. "I knew I was forgetting something. Here." A moment later, Scarlett's phone dinged with a message from the infomancer. She clicked on the link, and cameras from Provo appeared on her screen. "I've set up a feed that rotates through all the cameras for you. You can check whenever you like."

"You're the best."

The infomancer looked over her shoulder with a grin. "I know. Wish me luck."

"You don't need it. You have mad skills. Go kick them in the teeth, sister."

Amber pressed the buttons to enter her arming room, a featureless white space that extended endlessly in all directions. Her avatar wore a black suit with a white shirt, a narrow black tie, and polished black shoes. She'd recently upgraded the suit's defensive capabilities, which had proven to be a valuable improvement.

She waved to deploy several programs and pedestals rose out of the floor. They, too, were white and almost indistinguishable from their surroundings except for the objects on top of each. She retrieved the weapons first, three pistols of different sizes that she tucked into her jacket. They should've bulged the fabric but didn't since the jacket was bigger on the inside than it appeared from the outside.

Amber strapped on a silver wristwatch and added a ring on each hand. A small canister filled with spiders went on the back of her belt, and she added a few tiny grenades to small clips on the belt. She tucked a couple of other useful objects into her inside pockets, including lock breakers, analyzers, and the general tools of the infomancer trade that all avatars carried.

She considered her loadout against what she expected to go up against and added a small cylinder to the back of her belt and a pair of knives in forearm holders that would allow them to slide down into her hands with the right twist of her wrist.

Finally, she grabbed her sunglasses from the nearby pedestal and slipped them on. Data scrolled on both sides, giving her information about the items in her visual field, and small icons told her the status of her programs. She activated her basic defensive suite to call up shields, sensors, and basic speed-ups. After a last look to ensure she was ready, she rubbed her hands together in anticipation of the fights to come.

No matter how dangerous the real-world need that sent her into battle, no matter how important or unimportant the specific task at hand, every trip into the magical version of the dark web was an adventure that spoke to her soul. She grinned wide, spoke her borrowed catchphrase, "I make this look good," and rocketed out into the electronic landscape of the magical dark web.

CHAPTER SEVEN

Amber sped through the electronic cityscape and reveled in the blurred lights and colors around her. Being in her natural element was always liberating in a way she never experienced in her flesh body. Here, every part of her took in information like she was a giant sponge, and she reveled in the experience. As she scanned, she did so with purpose. She spotted her destination in short order, angled toward it, and dropped out of the sky to land in a crouch before straightening to regard the place.

The building ahead of her glowed in uniform white metal broken only by silver doors of various sizes set at ground level and a huge logo incorporating a turning gear that adorned the highest point of the front façade. She couldn't see how far back the structure extended from her angle but presumed the building would be enormous based on the visible portions.

Amber strode forward in search of a way in but spotted no doors of appropriate size for a person to use. Trucks pulled up and departed on a continuous basis, backing in so the trailer's rear aligned exactly with large silver plates mounted in the wall. She presumed that once the trucks were in place, the plates opened to allow the trucks to discharge their contents. As another truck backed in nearby, she laughed inwardly, muttered, "Well, why not?" and jumped onto the trailer's rear.

She activated her watch's magnetic field as she hit the back of the vehicle and her arm stuck to it, allowing her to keep her balance as the truck continued moving into position. As she'd expected, the silver gate flipped back and up into the building as the vehicle neared. She deactivated the magnet and jumped off as the truck's back gate rolled up, fell through the hole, and slid down the chute that led into the building. The slick surface quickly carried her down through complete darkness broken only by the red glow of scanning lasers.

Amber tumbled through another opening in the bottom and immediately rolled to the side and off the conveyor belt that would have carried her farther into the factory. She moved into the cover of a nearby piece of equipment. Boxes from the truck slid out of the chute and were carried along the conveyor belt to an intersection where some were directed one way, and the rest went the other.

The scale of the place was immense. She couldn't see the far wall, thanks to a combination of distance and several huge objects in between that occluded her view. The bottom floor of the building was covered with conveyor belts, machines of uncertain purpose, and motorized carts carrying things from one place to another. The carts had arms attached to lift their contents out, making them look uncomfortably like an unfortunate hybrid human.

The place was at least four stories high with multiple activity levels throughout its vertical space. A story above her, a grid supported wheeled claw-like appendages that would occasionally lower, grab something from the floor level, and transport it elsewhere. Other transports filled the space above it. Put simply, the place was pure chaos.

Her trained mind saw the simulation for what it was. The whole place was a reception area for data. The conveyors were analytical tools to route the data to where it needed to go, and the various pieces of equipment represented processes to manipulate the data before sending it onward.

Amber considered what standard defenses the infomancer who had coded the place would have installed. It only took her a moment to locate them. Cameras abounded. Their dark domed half-spheres showed in various corners and on every piece of equipment. Security robots marched around the ground level in pairs, their movements somehow less fluid than she would've expected from the quality of the rest of the simulation.

Usually, such occurrences meant the infomancer had borrowed the code for that portion of their program or modeled it after something that was out of place. She discarded the second option since she didn't recognize them from any movie or television show. The fact that they carried no obvious weapons made them an uncomfortable mystery.

Amber decided her best option was to avoid them entirely and pulled out a small device that would cast a holographic illusion over herself to make her seem like an ordinary part of the system. She tossed the object in the air, where it hovered for an instant before a small flying drone no larger than her hand whipped across in front of her face, curved, and slammed into the device, destroying itself and her projector.

She froze in shock and waited to see what would happen next. When no other action occurred, she muttered, "Okay. That's weird. Maybe the system recognizes technology but not me?" That didn't seem like a good explanation. But the robots kept marching, the conveyors kept conveying, and nothing else came out of the woodwork to attack her. With a shrug, she crossed the short distance from her current cover to one farther into the factory floor and waited again.

When that generated no response, she repeated the process until she'd covered about fifty feet and a security robot interposed itself in her way. Red and blue beams came out of small ports in its faceless head and scanned her up and down, then it swung a heavy arm at her head with impressive speed.

Fortunately, Amber was ready. She ducked the blow, drew her smallest pistol, and fired at the thing's feet. Needles stabbed through the appendages and into the floor. A moment later, they crackled with electricity. The current traveled up the robot's legs, through its torso, and into its head, which promptly exploded.

Amber managed to get an arm up in time so her reinforced black suit could catch the shrapnel flying at her face. She ran forward and hurdled the robot's remains as four more appeared out of nowhere to surround her. She shot the one blocking her forward progress in the face with the darts and the explosion detonated its head as well. Even that slight delay permitted more of them to close on her. She couldn't be fast enough to shoot them all before they got her.

Amber slipped her free hand into her jacket, grabbed her magnetic grapnel, and fired it up. It snagged onto a claw that was racing across the room and yanked her off her feet. She used the momentum to kick the nearest robot in the head and knocked it cartwheeling backward to crash down on a conveyor belt. It was carried into a large piece of equipment that exploded a moment later. Alarms sounded, and a bustle of activity occurred behind her.

She ignored it and focused entirely on the dangerous path ahead. Various claws carrying objects whipped across inches in front of her as she leaned from side to side to avoid them. Then she yanked the line to pull herself up to evade another. Finally, she disengaged the grapnel to prevent an imminent collision and landed hard, transitioning into a roll that slammed her against the side of a large metal cabinet.

Amber immediately surged to her feet and ran. The effort was fast enough to evade the attack of another type of security robot that shot at her from the gun barrels at the ends of its forearms. Laser blasts whipped past her and bullets slammed into her suit. She shot more enemies with the needle gun and was surprised when they went down, having half-expected they would adapt to her weapon. They hadn't, which made her think they were likely unsophisticated defense bots and not the real threat in the room.

Amber grabbed a grenade and tossed it behind her into the maw of another piece of equipment. Its explosion set off more chaos at her back. The next robot to appear before her had hands and gripped a large rifle. The weapon spat a huge bolt of energy at her that she only avoided by sliding onto her back on the floor, barely avoiding smacking her head on a pylon as she slipped under a conveyor belt.

She popped up and shot it, then growled a curse as the needle stuck in a force shield in front of the robot. Its sizzle of electricity accomplished nothing. Amber shoved the weapon into her jacket and grabbed her middle-sized pistol. This one fired bolts of energy at the robot. Her first shot struck the closest robot in the head and caused it to explode. The next one partially deflected the beam but went down anyway. The third one handled it easily with a new shield.

Amber grinned at the adaptation. "Think you're clever, do you?" She pressed the switch on the side of the pistol to change the kind of energy it emitted. A green blast shot out, penetrated the shield, and blew off the robot's head.

As she aimed at the next one, she suddenly flew across the room. She managed to collapse into a ball and cover her head before she slammed into a tower of boxes. It collapsed around her, and only her suit's improved resistance kept her from getting cut by the sharp edges of the metal containers. It didn't protect her hand, which took a nasty cut and forced her to pause, grab a healing pad from inside her jacket, and slap it on the wound.

In the real world, something had nibbled on her code and impaired her ability to interact with the simulation. It shouldn't be a problem right away, but it might become one over time, thus the patch.

Her awareness came back to her surroundings as three robots attacked at once. She shot one in the head, ducked under the bolt from another, and spun into a leg sweep on the third. Her shin slammed into the back of its legs and pain radiated up through her. The robot didn't move an inch from the blow.

She scrambled out of the way as it lifted its foot and stomped it down like a press onto where she'd been. She shot it, and its force field deflected the green blast. She switched to another kind of energy and fired, but its shield deflected it as it stomped toward her. "Damn, damn, damn."

Amber regained her feet and frantically looked around. She didn't want to pull her heaviest weapon because she hadn't yet made it that far into the system. She needed an alternative. She found it in a metal staircase that led up to a catwalk on the second floor. If she could get up there, she could access the higher stories, far away from the robots.

She grabbed a grenade, threw it to the floor, and used the blinding flash and deafening noise as a distraction to dart past the robot separating her from the metal stairs. The robot swung an arm at her that she easily avoided, and she wore a broad smile as she hit the staircase and took the steps three at a time.

The smile lasted only a few jumps before the staircase

flattened into a slide that offered no purchase as she slammed down onto it. She grasped futilely at the metal as she slid down. She flipped over on her back, expecting to see robots waiting, but instead saw a void in the floor at the bottom. A scream escaped her as she shot down through the hole into blackness.

CHAPTER EIGHT

The fall through space seemed like it would go on forever, then ended without transition. She didn't land. She was suddenly in a different place. A most unusual place, given where she'd come from. She muttered, "From twenty-second century to eighteenth in an instant."

The space appeared to be the entry room of a castle. Dark stone walls made of perfectly interlocking rocks with no visible mortar made up the perimeter walls. A sweeping staircase before her led up to the second floor where huge wooden doors stood open. To either side of the stairway were hallways leading toward the back of the first floor.

Ornate metal chandeliers hung from the ceiling and were filled with candles of differing heights as if they had burned at different rates. She nodded in appreciation to the designer for that touch. Symmetry was so often the default in things like this, and it took conscious effort to avoid it.

Ancient weapons, tall tapestries, and pieces of armor

and shields covered the walls. Narrow windows filled with metal and stained glass were cut at regular intervals all around the perimeter. The space was dim and chilly, physically and psychologically, radiating an aura of menace. She whistled, and the echo came back predictably, suggesting that what she saw wasn't an illusion within the simulation.

She had three options to select from and took a step toward the stairs, figuring up might lead to more interesting things. It had been trying to go up in the previous room that had delivered her here, so that theory might have flaws. A strange clattering sound from ahead and the sides caused her to backpedal. Skeletons marched into view with weapons gripped in their bony hands and individual pieces of armor positioned here and there on their yellowish-white bodies. They carried halberds, long handles with wicked axe heads on top.

Amber reacted instinctively, drawing her smallest pistol and shooting the first. The second shielded against the weapon. She shoved it into her pocket with a growl and ran to the wall. A double-ended spear was within her grasp. She jumped, snatched it from its mounting hooks, and spun it in front of her. In this space, any martial art she had researched was her own, thanks to the magic of computer programming, and she knew this one well.

She spun the weapon in both hands in front of her, the motion fast enough to deflect the halberds that slashed and stabbed in an effort to penetrate the defense. She flowed in a series of circles based on where her opponents moved, deftly keeping away from them and doing her best to narrow their ability to get behind her. She couldn't stay completely against the wall because focusing solely on defense would only increase how long it would take her to lose, not afford her a victory.

Amber assessed her opponents' moves to identify their weaknesses, then broke the pattern when one slashed at her. She stopped the spin of her spear, brought the bottom up under his halberd to redirect it into the skeleton next to him, then raised the other point and stabbed it horizontally through his rib cage. It slammed into his spine and severed it, causing the skeleton to drop in a jumble of bones as the one its halberd had hit did the same. She ran through where they'd been, jumping over the debris, and swept her spear down behind her to deflect additional attacks.

The skeletons didn't appear impressed by her fancy footwork as they continued to attack in the same fashion. She had their number now, and it took little time to eliminate them one by one until it was only her left in the room, panting and holding the halberd in high guard position. She lowered it, one point to the floor, and held it beside her. Her eyes narrowed as the sound of shuffling feet came to her, and she centered her focus in preparation for the next wave.

They turned out to be zombies instead of skeletons. Unfortunately, they weren't the easy, slow kind from the earliest films. They were the manic, animalistic, claws and teeth kind from the scarier movies that followed.

She reached into her jacket, pulled out the big pistol, and hit the button to extend it. Pieces bent and expanded to transform the weapon into a rifle, and she backpedaled as she shot the zombies one after the next. The first ten went down before they could reach her, but another ten had come in behind them, and they moved so fast she only managed to kill half of them before they reached hand-to-hand range.

She used the protection of her jacket to block slashes and punches, but one blow ripped through her cheek, and another injured her opposite hand. She heard the vague tone of a trace program activating and realized they'd wounded her enough to get through her first layer of defenses. She activated the blades in her shoes and used them to kick at the nearby zombies as she punched and flailed to gain some room. Then she slipped her hand behind her back, hit the lever to release her spiders, and grabbed the cylinder next to that container.

She activated the energy blade as she brought it around and whipped it into a horizontal strike that cut through all the zombies in front of her, chopping through their torsos with minimal effort. She met the third wave with her stylish attack, moving through kendo patterns with smooth precision as she chopped off arms, detached legs, and generally decapitated the horde of attackers. She was panting by the time they were all defeated, a sign of the increasing damage to her code.

No obvious opponent came as she stomped up the stairs with her anger at the situation and the damage she'd taken rising. When she reached the top and stepped through the doorway, she was in a long corridor. It had windows on each side of the same kind as the foyer, with more weapons, tapestries, and armor pieces on the walls. The floor was polished stone, and the same types of lights hung from above.

She noticed the flicker of the strange shadows a moment before she heard the wings. Huge bats flew at her, hundreds of them, filling the suddenly small-feeling space.

Amber slapped the cylinder back onto her belt, grabbed a pair of flash-bang grenades, and threw them on the floor. The bright flash did nothing against the bats, but the loud sound disoriented them and gave her a moment to ready herself for the attack. She tapped the rings she wore on her middle fingers together, then spread her arms apart. Large hands of force grew around her palms, as easy to move as her limbs but far larger and tougher.

She slapped the bats as they came near, punched a few, and clapped her hands around others, squashing them. She took a few bites as she defended herself against them, but the large hands made short work of that defense.

The next wave turned out to be mummies. She laughed when she saw their slow, shambling forms but sensed the disease in them, something that if injected into her code would probably immobilize her and allow the enemy to pick her apart if she stayed in the system.

She curled her fingers into fists and punched each mummy with her force magic fists. The impact propelled them out through the windows, up into the ceiling, or into the walls. None could get to her through the huge barrier, something she felt good about until it suddenly vanished, the energy of the program spent. She grabbed her middle pistol and fired it at the last one, hoping the levels of the defense didn't speak to one another. The mummy went down.

She called, "Pretty derivative. Castle. Monsters. What's next, gelatinous cubes?"

Laughter came from ahead. "Let's find out." Amber checked the status of her spiders and suppressed a curse. She had to give it to the infomancer who'd made this simulation and protected the server. They'd done good work.

Amber hadn't yet beaten his defenses, so she marched deeper into the lair. At the end of the corridor was a large dining room featuring a table with enough chairs to seat a dozen people that occupied the middle. More of the familiar chandeliers and wall decorations were in place.

A trio of figures in matching outfits stood beyond the table. Dark trousers, long black cloaks with red interiors, bright white shirts, and pendants at the neck. She groaned. "Vampires. Why did it have to be vampires?"

The one on the right laughed. "But vampires are so delicious."

The one in the center added, "We have—" He held up his hands to show the wicked talons that had replaced fingernails.

The last one finished, "Claws," and bared his teeth.

She drew her energy sword again. "And I have this. So, bring it on, corpses."

They attacked in unison, their movements so seamless that she was hard-pressed to defend herself. One would attack, and when she moved to the defense, another would attack in the spot she left open. She was forced to backpedal away from them and couldn't find or create an opportunity to counterattack. It occurred to her that she might be facing three infomancers instead of the one she'd assumed was controlling all three avatars.

Amber snarled and took a chance. She stopped backpedaling, feinted at the one on her right, then slashed across at the other two. The middle one leaned back fast enough, but she took the one on the other end by surprise when she lunged forward. The yellow energy beam pierced him through the heart, and he dissipated into pixels.

She whipped around defensively toward the others, but a hard strike on her arm caused her to lose the handle. The blade skittered across the floor and went out. The other two were on her instantly, and she backpedaled wildly and batted at their arms.

Amber twisted her wrists just so, and her knives slid out of their forearm sheaths into her hands. She cut the arms and hands that reached for her, which caused the vampires to slow their attack and become more cautious. It was still two against one, and in their system, they were faster than her.

Suddenly they paused, looked at each other, and smiled. Amber growled, "Oh, hell," as they came in again.

One leapt at her, and her only option was to twist and stab both knives into its throat. It fell backward and took her knives with it. The third one laughed in her ear as its teeth sank into her neck. She cried out in pain as it said in an almost loving caress, "You lose."

Amber tucked the grenades she'd grabbed into its waistband and dropped them. "You too." The ensuing blast killed the vampire and ejected her from the system. Back in the real world, Amber leaned back with a groan.

Behind her, Scarlett asked, "How'd it go?"

Amber didn't open her eyes. "Not well. I got beaten up."

Runeclaw interjected, "It's because we were here. Scarlett is bad luck."

Scarlett countered, "Jerk."

Runeclaw laughed. "Notice that she's not saying I'm wrong."

Amber shook her head. "I need a drink. It'll take a while for my bots to decode whatever my spiders were able to pull out of the system. You're buying."

Scarlett laughed. "Seems fair. Let's go."

CHAPTER NINE

The next day, Scarlett got to the warehouse early and looked around for ways to make herself useful. She discovered Lin sitting on the floor in the equipment area surrounded by pieces of gear. Scarlett dropped to sit cross-legged beside the drow, and Runeclaw plopped himself between them, lying like a loaf with his paws tucked under his body. Scarlett asked, "What are we doing?"

Lin replied, "Fixing, mending, polishing. The usual."

"You do this all the time?"

"Pretty much. Every time we go out and get in a fight, someone needs to make sure everything's set back to normal. In general, that someone is me."

Scarlett lifted a coil of wire and examined it. "Why you?"

Lin took the coil away from her. "I've got a gift for the details. And I enjoy it. Totally Zen."

Runeclaw interjected, "It requires brainpower, so Scarlett wouldn't understand."

She patted his head gently, then flicked his ear with the snap of her finger. "Jerk."

Lin asked, "Want to learn?"

"Sure."

At the same moment, Runeclaw countered, "She's not capable of it."

Scarlett flicked his ear again. "Shut it, you."

Lin handed over a pistol and grabbed another from the floor beside her. She ordered, "Pop the magazine." Scarlett did so. "Rack the slide."

Scarlett complied with that as well. "What next?"

"Now we take it apart, clean every piece, and put it back together."

They chatted as they worked, and eventually Scarlett asked, "Why aren't you using magic for this? Seems like some of it would be easier that way, especially the delicate stuff."

Lin shrugged. "It's intricate work with magic, which requires a lot of concentration and focus. I can do it this way in my sleep. Besides, there's something nice about the tactile feel of working with your hands, don't you think?"

Scarlett agreed, and someone behind them replied, "Definitely." They looked over their shoulders and saw Amber with three cups of coffee. She set two down and kept one for herself as she sat behind Runeclaw and yawned. "Excuse me. Long night."

Lin replied, "Working or playing?"

The infomancer poked her arm. "Working. Which you already know."

"One can always hope you might find something other than work to occupy your life."

"Right back at you."

Lin laughed. "I'm too busy for anything other than work now that Scarlett's around."

Scarlett replied, "Hey, not nice."

Amber countered, "But accurate."

Scarlett asked, "So, worker bee, find out anything interesting?"

Amber grunted in annoyance. "No. My spiders have decoded three-fourths of the data and so far it's useless nonsense. There's still a bit of hope, but it's dwindling fast."

"So, what do we do now?"

Amber shrugged. "We wait for Trane to do something useful, I guess, at least until our trace drops off him."

Scarlett figured that made sense. "And then?"

"Pick him up, I suppose."

Lin snapped a piece of her pistol together with an audible *click*. "Now you're talking. Why bother waiting?"

Amber replied, "Because he might lead us somewhere useful without knowing he was doing it. Which is probably better than whatever he'd give us while you were beating him up."

"But beating him up would be a reward in its own right."

Amber rose, stretched, and shook her head at Lin. "One track mind, you. Let's go for subtlety on this one, okay?"

As the infomancer wandered away, Lin called, "Subtlety is overrated." Amber waved in response.

Scarlett grumbled, "I hate all this waiting around."

"Me too."

"We could always go after the watchers in Provo or

Austin, I suppose. They won't know anything more than the other two did, though."

Lin worked the slide on the pistol to check it. "True. And they were useless idiots, to boot."

Runeclaw commented, "If our signal is dwindling, I could always sneak into Trane's house again to reapply the tracker."

Scarlett replied, "I like the idea of picking him up more."

The cat sniffed. "Of course you do. Always opting for brawn over brains."

Lin slapped her hands down on her thighs. "Okay. We'll eat ourselves alive if we keep this up. Let's go riding."

Twenty minutes later, they'd returned all the gear to where it belonged, grabbed some necessities for the road, and headed out of town on their motorcycles. Scarlett and Lin chatted over comms as they rode, trading the lead now and again as one or the other decided to push the pace. Traffic was light and the beautiful day was perfect for riding aimlessly.

After several hours, as the sun was beginning to go down, they entered a large forest. Lin pulled off onto a path on the right. The ride turned bumpy as they traveled over gravel and dirt, finally ending in a clearing. Lin parked her bike and climbed off. Scarlett did the same and asked, "Where are we?"

"Hunters camp out here during the season. There's a stream nearby, an abundant supply of wood already chopped, and lots of areas for a tent. Feel like staying over?"

"Sure." They'd brought bedrolls and basic camping

supplies in case such an opportunity presented itself. They cleared the area with magic, using bursts of force to brush away debris and levitate rocks and such out of the way.

Lin offered, "Let me show you a trick." She took a small tin out of her bag and opened it to reveal a waxy blue substance. She walked around the perimeter gathering stones, daubed each with the blue wax, and set it down in a large oval that covered a third of the clearing. When she finished, she snapped her fingers.

Scarlett felt a force barrier appear to create a dome over them.

The drow grinned. "Instant tent."

Scarlett laughed. "Very nice. So much easier than the normal kind."

"Takes up less space, too." Lin opened a portal, reached through, and pulled out a cooler.

"Did you plan this stayover?"

"No, but I called back and asked someone to pull stuff together for us once I realized how the timing was working out. Go ahead and start a fire. Let's make some food."

Scarlett soon had a nice fire blazing, fed by some deadwood she'd gathered, opting not to take what was already cut. They cooked and ate, then leaned back with cups of coffee laced with whiskey and looked up at the stars. Runeclaw ran around the clearing in a series of mad dashes that ended with leaps into the air to swat at glowing bugs.

Scarlett commented, "Fireflies. One of those things that are the same here as on Oriceran."

Lin replied, "Except we call them lightning bugs."

"Really?"

"Really."

Scarlett frowned. "Why?"

The other woman laughed. "Why do you call them fireflies? They're not on fire, nor, I believe, are they flies."

"They're not using lightning either."

The drow sounded triumphant. "Ha. But they *are* bugs. Which puts me one better than you."

Scarlett shook her head. "You're an idiot."

Lin called, "Are you actually trying to catch those things, Runeclaw, or just scare them?"

"Catch them. They have an exquisite cronch."

Scarlett made a face. "Ew. Gross, I did not need to know that."

Lin leaned back on her elbows and returned her gaze to the heavens. "So. What are you going to do once this thing with the Veil is over?"

Scarlett matched the other woman's position. "If you'd asked me this morning, I wouldn't have had an answer. After today? I think I'll ride for a while. See where the road takes me."

"That sounds glorious."

Scarlett turned her head to look at the other woman. "You should come along."

Lin looked back with a smile. "Maybe I will."

Runeclaw made a scampering sound that drew both of their attention, and they watched as he continued to chase the fireflies or lightning bugs. Scarlett laughed. "We can find a magical cat for you too."

The other woman groaned. "No, I'm good."

"A bird then."

"Nothing that talks. I don't need a constant assault on my self-esteem, thanks."

Runeclaw jumped, landed awkwardly, then stood and ran after another lightning bug like he'd meant to do exactly that. Scarlett laughed at his antics. "But look at the fun you're missing out on."

The other woman shook her head. "Still no."

"Your loss." Scarlett looked up at the stars. *Yeah, this is something I could do for a while.*

CHAPTER TEN

Camus entered his sitting room ten minutes before the meeting time to get himself settled. He had been taking it easy, hoarding his magical, physical, and mental energies, and not stressing himself by rushing in at the last minute was part of that effort. Overall, events were not progressing as he'd planned, although the trackers had been a bit of inspiration that had worked out even better than expected.

The gathering was not far off. Those pieces were falling into place exactly as he expected, yet he couldn't fully block out his fear that such success might be exceedingly temporary. His tenure as the leader of the Veil had been an excellent one by any measure. He had made positive steps on behalf of the organization, increasing power for him, and extracted the weak links through attrition or by his hand.

He would've preferred not to have lost one of his reliable pair of underlings, but his enemies were skilled. It did him no good to pretend they weren't since denial wouldn't change the fact of their interference. After tonight, they would hopefully no longer be something to worry about.

He had barely settled himself in the chair when a servant came in with the tray. It held only one mug alongside the silver carafe of coffee. He didn't intend the meeting to last long. A plate of fruit and nut bars sat beside it.

The man poured, and Camus nodded his thanks as he lifted the cup to his lips. A sip helped to center him so he could fully enjoy the taste of the second sip. Coffee was a mind-calming ritual for him. He had many of them and had spent a significant amount of time in his downstairs sanctuary of late, his most powerful refuge. No negativity touched him there.

Today, events that required his presence were in motion. The die was about to be cast, and he wanted to know the results as quickly as possible. A scuff from the entrance drew his attention to the man who had entered. Ellis already wore his combat uniform, but not with body armor, weapons, and so forth. Only the base black layer, heavy boots, and the like.

Camus nodded. "Ellis. Good to see you. Is everything prepared?"

The other man nodded. "Yes. We are ready."

"Explain."

"Both teams are ready to move but are not yet deployed at the location. We have very high-altitude drone surveillance, distant enough to ensure safety but not so distant that we can't use it. We'll bring them closer during the operation, of course. Would you like to watch firsthand? I can arrange a feed."

Camus shook his head. "No. Updates from you will be sufficient. Continue."

"We anticipate overwhelming force. The strike should come as a total surprise, but even if it doesn't, we're bringing a lot of firepower to the party."

"Magicals?"

"Yes."

Camus frowned. "But not from inside the Veil or your security force."

Ellis straightened at this hint of criticism. "No, sir. No one from inside, other than me. Freelancers."

"And our fighters?"

"The same. Mercenaries from several organizations."

Camus took a bar from the plate and nibbled at it. "No chance of anything being traced back to us?"

Ellis offered a small shrug. "Only to me, and I'm just a voice on the phone up until the moment I join the troops. The company knows me, but none of the rank and file should. Our infomancers are sure we're fine in that regard. I'll wear a mask or illusion that obscures my features."

Camus delayed for another sip of his coffee. "You'll ensure everything is in perfect order before giving the instruction to go?"

"I will. And I'll watch throughout the operation."

"Keep me informed as you think appropriate, but err for more rather than less."

Ellis nodded. "Yes, sir."

Camus smiled. "Good hunting, my friend."

After leaving Camus, Ellis had spent the rest of the day working on things related to the gathering. His role in the night's events wasn't particularly active or dangerous since he'd hired quality people and intended to let them do their jobs. His presence would only be as an observer and a resource for the mission commanders. He would be armed, and if he spotted the witch through the scope of his rifle, he would pull the trigger and be grateful for the opportunity.

He had told one small untruth to Camus since the fact had slipped his mind. One other member of his organization, the magical who assisted him most often, would join him tonight. He would need transport at a moment's notice, and the man was currently out making sure he knew the destination and had safe areas of retreat nearby.

His subordinate overseeing security for the gathering entered the room. "Should you really be doing this?" It was the third time she'd asked.

He smiled and gave her the same answer as before. "Yes." This time, he explained, "It's essential that I know what's going on. Any clue that might drop. Any piece of knowledge about our enemies."

"So, you don't think tonight will be decisive?"

He pulled a coin from his desk drawer and spun it, his personal stress management habit. As he watched it twirl, he replied, "I hope it will be. I *think* it will be. But I don't *know* that it will be, and that makes all the difference. So, I'll prepare like this won't take care of the problem and do what I can to mitigate any future issues."

She smiled and put a hand on her hip. "You know what mitigates a lot of problems? Missiles."

Ellis laughed. "I think I suggested the same thing. Magical defenses can sometimes deal with such things, so it's not the safest bet."

A frown grew on her features. "All in all, I'd be fine with a world without magic."

He checked his watch and rose. "Yeah, there would be a lot to be said for that. That's not the world we live in, so no point in worrying about it."

She walked with him as he headed out and they continued the conversation until he arrived at his transport waiting outside.

The wizard asked, "Ready to go, boss?"

Ellis replied, "You're going to take us somewhere secluded?"

"Of course, boss. Not my first rodeo."

"Let's do it." A moment later, he was in a wooded area about a half-mile from the bar the Witches on Wheels owned and frequented. The leader of the mercenaries, visible as such by a glow-in-the-dark stripe on the back of his helmet, bustled up to them. Ellis asked, "Everything good?"

The other man nodded. "Both teams are ready, just waiting on your word to get this party started."

"What have you seen?"

"We've got an outer perimeter about a tenth of a kilometer outside the building. Some stragglers a little farther out, probably there as early warning, but we'll sweep them up as we get started."

"No sign that they noticed you?"

"None."

Ellis smiled. Perfect. "Magic defenses?"

The man scratched the side of his neck. "Our magicals and infomancers have scanned like crazy. About the defenses you'd expect, both magical and mundane. We'll deal with them."

Ellis nodded at the expected answer. They were paying these men a lot, yet he had very little doubt about their quality. He ran through his concerns and hopes in his mind, then asked, "What do you need from me?"

The man replied, "Stay on comms in case we have a question. Otherwise, keep yourself safe. I want you as a reference for people thinking about hiring us in the future."

Ellis laughed. "That confident, are you?"

"You know it. Soon, you'll know why."

"All right then. We'll hang out back here. The operation is in your capable hands."

The man nodded, turned, and walked toward Wheels. Over the comms, he announced, "One minute. Incoming. Forward teams, standby."

CHAPTER ELEVEN

That night, Scarlett sat at a round table in Wheels with Lin, Amber, and Runeclaw. The place was busy, filled with Witches and locals alike, but it didn't have the carefree vibe of the first days she'd spent there. By Wren's order, all the Witches were armed and were careful with their indulgence.

Ever since the first attack on the place, there'd been a focus on handling another one if the enemy got clever again. Scarlett thought if it were going to come it would've already happened but knew better than to argue with Wren. She wasn't carrying a pistol, but her wand was up her sleeve. Fang rode inside her jacket, and her earpiece was in its usual spot.

Now and again, a murmur from an unfamiliar voice reported on the status of the defenses. The extra security they'd hired seemed confident and capable.

Amber commented, "I think I like the name lightning bugs better."

Scarlett shrugged. "Fireflies. Lightning bugs. Whatever. Still seems gross to me."

Runeclaw smugly replied, "Exquisite cronch."

Scarlett patted him on the head condescendingly. "Yes, yes, we know. It's always strange to see you acting like a cat."

"That's because your brain doesn't work right."

Scarlett frowned. "Rude."

Before Runeclaw could reply, Wren yelled, "Quiet." Conversations inside Wheels stilled as Scarlett winced. Wren's voice had been very loud over the comms.

A moment later, someone from the team outside growled, "Blitz, blitz, blitz."

Scarlett shot up from the table an instant before Lin did the same and headed toward the back door. The Witches had been divided into teams. Each had an area of responsibility should an attack happen. Blitz was the warning that something worthy of further active defenses had occurred.

From the corner of her eye, she saw Amber and Runeclaw hurry toward the nearest group of civilians. They would handle moving them into a back room and portaling them to the safety of the warehouse.

As they got outside, Scarlett commented, "I can't believe the Veil would be dumb enough to attack here again."

Their willingness to do so became evident a moment later as fireballs arced out of the surrounding trees to rain down toward the building. Scarlett snapped up shields that overlapped with those of the defenders nearest her and pumped magical energy into them as she added some to her muscles and senses. The flames struck the shields and dissipated harmlessly.

A moment later, the chatter of gunfire filled the night. Metal plates had been positioned strategically around the building in anticipation of such a thing. Scarlett twitched her wand to raise several of them in front of herself, Lin, and the next nearest Witch. Again, defenses overlapped as others did the same.

The enemy was invisible, which made counterattacking difficult. Witches fired their guns blindly toward the source of incoming rounds, and while they were occasionally rewarded with a cry of pain, the enemy still maintained their magical invisibility.

Scarlett growled, "What I wouldn't give for a giant antimagic emitter right now."

Lin countered, "Says the woman who didn't bring a pistol to the gunfight."

"I know where my strengths lie."

Wren announced, "Initiate phase one." Scarlett and Lin expectantly turned their heads toward the enemy, and a moment later, a series of explosions sounded all around the building.

Ellis automatically crouched at the sound of the explosions even though they were far ahead of him, near where his troops were positioned for their attack. The commander reported, "Minimal damage. Shields held, except where we stood right on top of the explosives."

"Still good to go?"

"Yes, sir."

Ellis clapped him on the shoulder. "Very good. Time for the next surprise."

The commander nodded and snapped, "Drones." The word was a command.

Ellis looked up and saw eight drones whip by overhead. They had been circling high above in a holding pattern that allowed them to maintain surveillance on the area around the building. Now, they'd formed up into their pre-planned attack run. Infomancers would be operating them, but the task was simple enough that they could have done it with the onboard systems.

He selected one to watch in his display and got a view from the small camera in the nose. It zoomed across the ground in only a few seconds and activated the rotary cannon in its nose. Bullets stitched the ground and intersected the line of defenders. Their magical shields did nothing to protect them since his people exclusively used anti-magic ammunition for this battle. The pieces of metal, already pocked with hits from other bullets, held fast in most cases. A couple of rounds got through, and at least one witch went down with a head wound that looked like it might be fatal.

The defenders' discipline held and might have made him frown if the screen hadn't flared with the launch of the missiles. He remarked, "This should be good."

Wren snarled, "Defend above."

On each team, one person was the attacker and one was

the defender. Scarlett looked up and saw the drones highlighted in her glasses. One of them pulsed with color as Amber gave her a specific target. She blasted the drone with lightning, and as it spiraled out of the sky, her pulsing target shifted to an incoming missile. The projectile descended fast toward Wheels, giving Scarlett only one shot to intercept it.

She threw out a burst of fire shaped into a cone for a better chance of success. It intersected the missile. Instead of exploding as she'd expected, the projectile broke open and discharged a thick vapor. It swirled around for several moments before catching fire and dropping toward Wheels like gravity pulled it. The fiery stuff landed on the overlapping shields protecting the building and continued to burn.

More missiles were intercepted or struck and broke open on the shield to add more fire to the stuff already burning on their protective layer. The sound of explosions came from the front of the building, and Scarlett winced. "I'm glad Dusk Runner's at the warehouse."

Lin nodded. "Same with mine."

Wren growled, "Dammit. I don't know what they used, but it starts as a gas. Defenders, drop the upper shields and blow the fires away from the building and onto the highway or into a clearing."

Scarlett complied, beginning her force breeze before she released her section of shield. She sent the fiery vapor flying toward a clearing that would hopefully be safe from additional explosions or other hazards. Beside her, Lin observed, "They came to play hard. Not good."

Ellis grinned at the sound of the motorcycles exploding. It was a deeply satisfying song. Now that they were on their heels, it was time to layer on more. "Nice one. Keep it going."

The commander ordered, "Initiate second assault. Primary team, advance."

Scarlett's display got busier as motion and magic sensors around the building lit up. The enemy was on the move.

Wren commanded, "Rock 'n' roll."

Scarlett laughed as she had when she first heard the command and what it entailed, then used her magic to lift the gravel placed in strategic piles around the building. They had painted it with a substance that glowed in her display. She threw it out in a straight line parallel to the ground, covering about ten to fifteen degrees of arc. Other Witches did the same on both sides to create a circle of gravel fanning out from the center.

The veils hiding their enemies were good, but when the gravel stopped because it hit a shield, it revealed their location. Beside her, Lin's rifle went off in bursts of three bullets. The Witches were all using anti-magic ammunition, knowing the Veil had magic on their side, so all the shooters would be conservative with their barrages.

Soldiers became visible as they fell to the ground, wounded or dead, providing the first view of their enemy. The attackers wore body armor and carried heavy weapons, which to Scarlett's mind meant they were mercenaries.

The enemy magicals kept up the veils where they could and threw magical attacks at the defenders. Scarlett was hard-pressed to continue throwing out the gravel to identify new threats, preserve the metal barriers in front of those she was protecting, and keep her magical shields solid in front and above. The constant gunfire gave her a headache, and she wished she could be one of the offensive team members rather than focused on defending them.

After an amount of time she couldn't measure, the gunfire slackened as if the enemy had halted their advance and wanted to maintain the existing balance. Scarlett asked, "Why did they stop?"

The answer came an instant later as Wren announced, "Warehouse is under attack."

Lin growled, "How the hell did they find it?"

Wren replied, "Doesn't matter. Even teams, fall back into Wheels and portal to the warehouse. Odd teams, keep up our defenses." Lin and Scarlett ran for the door into Wheels and the next fight that awaited them.

CHAPTER TWELVE

The inside of Wheels was empty except for a portal being held open by a couple of Witches in the corner. Scarlett ran toward it, and Runeclaw jumped onto her shoulder from his position on the bar. He said, "Everyone's away safe."

She replied, "But not safe. They're attacking the warehouse." He snarled something she was pretty sure was a curse in a language she didn't understand as she ran through the portal into the warehouse.

The building bustled with activity as Witches turned over beds to create impromptu cover while others focused on setting up shields and defenses inside. They hadn't anticipated an attack on the warehouse, so it didn't have more than standard-level defenses. Scarlett wondered how the mercenaries discovered the place but couldn't imagine what the answer might be. It wasn't immediately important anyway.

The sounds of battle drew her toward an outer door, and she slammed her shoulder into it and catapulted through. The similarity to the fight she'd left was astonishing. Drones flew overhead and launched missiles. They erupted into flames that gushed onto the defenders' shields above the building.

Unfortunately, these shields weren't as carefully put together as the ones outside Wheels had been. She threw up hers in vulnerable spots as she assessed the situation. Lin remarked, "I've only got one mag left. I'll focus on defense. You go cause trouble."

Scarlett stepped into the shadows and cast a veil around herself and another around Runeclaw. Together, they moved away from the building and the direction the attack came from, then circled back toward it. Scarlett flicked her display glasses to show thermal signatures but still didn't see anything. She whispered, "Amber, can you give me anything out here?"

The infomancer replied, "I've got all our detectors wide open. Whoever did the veils on these guys are damn good. And we don't have any handy gravel prepositioned at the warehouse."

Scarlett searched the area and smiled when she saw a pile of construction materials. The Witches had been working on fixing one side of the warehouse and had stacked their supplies under a tarp. With a twitch of her wand, she removed the tarp, turned over the containers of screws and nails, and shook them until all their contents were free. Then she used her magic to throw the projectiles out in a semicircle. Once again, some projectiles stopped and indicated where veiled figures stood.

Runeclaw hissed, "I've got the one on the right."

Scarlett nodded. "I'll take the one on the left. Good hunting. Be careful."

He snorted. "You're the one who's danger-prone."

Runeclaw stayed low to the ground as he moved forward. The area he passed through was more dirt than vegetation, but some scattered low grass and weeds let him stay more or less concealed.

He imagined his target had changed location after being targeted with the nails and screws, but that didn't matter. His senses were keen at all times, and especially so where veiled enemies were involved. It was as if he could smell the magic that hid them, but it only worked for that kind of magic. Fortunately, he didn't need to understand how it worked to use it.

He crawled close enough to get inside the veil and saw a soldier with a wizard standing behind him. They spotted Runeclaw at the same moment he did them. The soldier yelped as he fumbled his weapon and the wizard swiped his wand around.

Runeclaw jumped onto the soldier's chest, putting the man between himself and the magical. His claws did no damage as they sank into the bulletproof vest, but he gathered his muscles and propelled himself up.

When his claws sank in again, it was into the flesh of the man's cheeks and the sides of his neck. Runeclaw would've chosen the eyes as a target, but the man's goggles prohibited it. Still, the soldier screamed, dropped his weapon, and lifted his hands toward his face as Runeclaw carved more deep furrows into his flesh.

Before the man could grab him, Runeclaw launched himself again, this time to the top of the man's head. He was shocked as a force blast from the wizard struck him.

The shield Scarlett still had around him countered most of the impact, but it was great enough to knock him from his perch. He twisted in midair, landed clean on the ground, and ran between the wizard's legs. Another force blast slammed into the ground behind him, but it wasn't quick enough to catch him.

The wizard spun in place, but Runeclaw dashed back toward the soldier who was still distracted by his wounds and slashed at the back of the wizard's legs. He had no armor protecting his calves, and Runeclaw's claws sank deep into the muscle and tore it.

The wizard screamed as his leg collapsed, and when he hit the ground, Runeclaw was on him again. He slashed across the man's eyes, but the man ducked, and his claws raked the wizard's forehead. Blood flowed, and Runeclaw jumped down to the man's hand and savagely bit the fingers holding the wand.

The man released it and wrenched his body around, one hand coming down to smash the cat flat, but Runeclaw was already out of the way. He finished both enemies with a blast of lightning from his tail, making sure they'd be out for a while, then dashed away as a fireball blasted past his head.

Scarlett felt the touch of Fang's mind the instant her hand closed around the hilt. The dagger was eager for combat but didn't have the same pushy presence it had before. The renegotiation of their relationship was holding for the moment. She whispered, "Can you help me find these bastards?"

Fang replied in her mind, *I sense a presence ahead to the left.*

Scarlett angled in that direction, her reflexes primed to react. She didn't find anyone until the moment she bumped into him. His veil was tight to his body, just as hers was to hers. The hot barrel of his rifle burned the skin of her left hand, but she ignored it and brought her right hand around to smash the gun away from her.

The veil stayed in place, so she maintained contact with him by grabbing a bunch of fabric in her fist. She whipped her damaged hand up in a ridge hand strike to his face, her thumb tucked under to protect it, and cursed as she connected with his chin. That blow was much better against vulnerable areas and hurt like hell when you missed.

She switched responsibilities and grabbed the front of his shirt with her left hand. She leaned back, chambered her arm, and whipped a vicious elbow strike around at the same level.

He must've felt it coming because he fell to the ground, wrenching himself out of her grip. She jumped instinctively to the side and felt the passage of his legs underneath her as he tried to sweep them out. She landed and went to the ground, reaching out and finding his helmet. She shoved it forward to try to push it over his eyes and blind him, then landed a punch to his kidneys.

His back arched, and she felt him wrench around. Knowing she had him in the right spot, she sank Fang into his leg. He stiffened instantly. Then his body slackened under her as the tranquilizing poison took effect.

Scarlett panted, and Fang asked, *Why didn't you just stab him from the outset?*

She climbed to her feet and brushed dirt off herself. "Didn't want to kill him. Might want to ask him some questions later. Since I couldn't see him, that was a problem."

Next one is forward to your left again. A little farther away.

Scarlett mumbled, "So annoying." She went in that direction, found the soldier, and took him out with a straight thrust as soon as she felt his arm. A flicker of magic told her the wizard was nearby, and she charged in that direction. Her shield slammed into another. Then she could see the wizard.

He blasted her with lightning magic, but her shield held. She stabbed down at him with Fang, but the dagger failed to get through the multiple layers of shields protecting him. Scarlett punched him in the face, but that didn't make it through his defenses either.

Then he staggered forward as paws came around his face and scratched his eyes. The distraction gave her an opening, and she stabbed him to put him to sleep. Runeclaw jumped on her shoulder before the wizard fell.

She whispered, "Nice job."

He replied, "These people are idiots."

"Agree."

A voice in her ear ordered, "Scarlett, fall back. We've been pushed into the warehouse."

She turned and ran, then launched herself through a window. It shattered, causing those nearby to flinch toward her. When they saw who she was, they returned their attention to a huge breach in the far wall where grenades had given the enemy ingress. Magic and bullets were holding the attackers out, but not particularly well.

After a moment, shouts came from the other side as the enemy called, "The witch." They pointed at her.

Lin quipped, "Well, I guess you're popular with someone, anyway."

Runeclaw added, "Couldn't have said that better myself."

A moment later, anti-magic emitters activated, and all their physical and magical shields fell. Lin snapped, "They're after you. Run."

Scarlett ran.

CHAPTER THIRTEEN

Scarlett pelted through the door and into the combat outside. She focused on keeping her feet moving and not tripping over anything. The green-tinted display was a help and a hindrance, rendering the night into the strangest shapes and colors. Runeclaw hissed and snarled as he ran at her side and occasionally warned of enemies ahead.

Amber advised through her earpiece, "You've drawn off several attackers."

A bullet whizzed past her ear, and Scarlett flinched away from it. "How many is that, exactly?"

"About a third of them."

"Fantastic. So glad I could be of help." She leapt to avoid a root and twisted her ankle as she came down. She ignored the pain and pushed on, bending into a lower crouch as more bullets swept through the air around her. "Can you isolate who has the anti-magic emitter?" If she could get shields up or put some barriers around her, that would be something.

"No. Overlapping fields, unfortunately. There are at least three trailing you, possibly more."

"Damn it. Whoever is responsible for creating portable anti-magic emitters needs to be slapped. Hard."

A slight sizzle sounded at her side but quickly cut off. Runeclaw felt the same bump of magic returning for an instant that she had. Whoever trailed her was as fast and at least as good as she was in the forest. The possibility of at least three people triangulating on her with anti-magic emitters was concerning, and she wasn't sure how to change the odds in her favor. Her flight might not continue for long if she didn't find a way.

Amber instructed, "Veer left, toward the road."

Scarlett complied without question. A moment later, a fierce burning in her leg told her she'd been shot. The limb collapsed underneath her, and she went down in the dirt. Rocks and tree roots ripped her hands as she caught herself. She pushed the pain to the back of her mind with the twisted ankle, got to her feet, and continued limping in the same direction.

She shoved Fang into a pocket and gripped her thigh with her hand. She was that much slower now, which meant they would catch her faster.

The thought had barely crossed her mind when a man ran into view, closing at an angle from her left. Runeclaw skidded to go after him, and Scarlett wished she had a gun.

Before they could take any further action, the loud growl of an engine sounded, and a motorcycle hurtled through the air out of the nearby tree line. Scarlett recognized it instantly as Dusk Runner and felt a grim hope for her escape as the bike slammed into the man who'd been closing on them and knocked him flying. The bike stopped, waiting for them.

She ran forward, caught Runeclaw when he jumped up, braced her legs on either side, and snapped, "Go."

The motorcycle pulled out in a spray of dirt from the back tire, remotely piloted by Amber. Scarlett leaned forward as far as she could and fished around in her jacket with her free hand until she found her healing potion. She uncapped it and waited. After fifteen seconds, she was confident they'd left the anti-magic emitters behind. She drank the potion and gritted her teeth as it healed her wounds.

Scarlett shoved the empty vial into her inner pocket, pulled out her wand, activated the bike's enchantments, and created the force band for Runeclaw to grab onto. She shoved the wand back in her sleeve and gripped the handlebars. "Should I come back to the warehouse?"

Lin replied, "No. We're knocking them back. The attack at Wheels is over, and we have more defenders here." Although all that sounded like good news to Scarlett, Lin's tone was dark.

Scarlett replied, "Good, good."

Amber warned, "What's not good is the eight drones coming in at you."

A tactical map opened in Scarlett's display glasses, showing her motorcycle in the lead and eight small X shapes flying behind. As they neared her, they opened up with machine guns, and she slewed the bike left and right to avoid getting hit. Amber reported, "They're committed to the attack."

Scarlett replied, "Perfect. Hold on." She slammed on the motorcycle's brakes and focused on not going over the handlebars as the bike screeched to a halt. The drones flew past too fast to react to her move.

Amber commented, "You're lucky they didn't launch missiles. You'd be toast."

"That's what shields are for." She gunned the engine and lined up the targeting reticules in her display with two of the drones that were slowing to turn around. She hit the launch button and the missile pod on the front of her bike disintegrated as the two missiles shot out. She trusted them to do their jobs and drew her wand from her sleeve. A dozen fireballs nailed two more drones, leaving her with four to go.

They faced her now, and the distance between them closed at an almost terrifying rate. Scarlett threw more fireballs and managed to take out one. Another continued straight at her, and two more leapt around to either side, intent on getting out of range of her attacks and coming in for a better angle.

A missile shot out of the drone, and Scarlett smashed it with a wave of force. It exploded and shot shrapnel down toward the motorcycle. Her shields caught it, but then bullets slammed into Dusk Runner's body.

Scarlett wrenched the front wheel to the side, taking the motorcycle out of the path of the bullets, and the missile shot by. She stopped the bike, breathed slowly for a couple of seconds, then gunned the engine again. Two were on their way in, with one behind and turning. Scarlett advised, "I can get the near ones."

Amber replied, "I can get the far one."

Scarlett wrenched the front wheel around again to head away from the incoming drones. At her side, the drone compartment opened, and the drone lifted out. It was quickly lost from her vision, but she saw the feed in her glasses. Amber used it as a projectile to take out the rearmost drone, leaving Scarlett with only two more to deal with.

Runeclaw asked, "Are you sure this is a good idea?"

She laughed. "It's an excellent idea. Prepare to blast." She hit the button and watched the distance close, then wove the bike again to avoid the incoming bullets. When they were close enough, she hit the button to release the caltrops, then twisted and leaned back.

She lifted the sharp metal triangles into the air and sent them toward the incoming drones in a cloud. She snapped, "Now," and Runeclaw blasted electricity out of his tail to energize the metal bits. The drones struck that combination of velocity and energy and immediately detonated. Scarlett slowed the bike, then stopped it. "We good?"

Amber confirmed, "Yeah, you're set."

Scarlett used her wand to open a portal near the warehouse and rolled Dusk Runner through it. She parked the bike and crept toward the remaining sounds of combat. A small group of attackers were still harrying the opening in the side. Scarlett and Runeclaw snuck up behind them and took them out with a combination of claws and Fang.

Lin came out from the building. "You all right?"

Scarlett nodded. "Yeah, I'll live. Dusk Runner's got some scratches and scrapes, so Maddox will yell at me, but I'll live."

The drow shook her head. "You're so irresponsible."

"I know."

Lin clapped her on the shoulder. "Come with me. We'll make a sweep, make sure all of these bastards are down or gone."

CHAPTER FOURTEEN

After helping clear up the warehouse because she was told she wasn't needed at Wheels, Scarlett portaled back to the hotel and fell into bed, exhausted. The next morning, when her brain was functioning again, she portaled to the warehouse. It was unexpectedly empty with only a couple of Witches left on guard. She asked, "Where is everybody?"

"Wheels. Or, more accurately, what's left of it."

Scarlett frowned and opened a portal to the parking lot in front of the tavern. She realized then why Lin's voice had sounded strange the night before when she'd said the battle at Wheels was over. Scarlett hadn't realized that meant they'd lost it.

The building was a shambles. At least half of it had burned away, and scorch marks and burns covered the rest. The roof had caved in over half the place.

Lin walked up to her, put her index finger on Scarlett's chin, and pushed her mouth closed. "Yeah, the old place is not a pretty sight."

Scarlett frowned. "I didn't realize what you meant last night."

"I didn't want you to. You had enough to think about."

"Why?"

The other woman shrugged. "Wren decided we needed to focus all our efforts on defending people at the warehouse. It was the right call."

"Quite a price, though." The deep voice behind her made Scarlett turn, and she smiled at the sight of Maddox and a bunch of Spell Riders rolling up on their motorcycles. Behind them were several flatbed trucks with lumber and other supplies stacked on them.

Maddox stepped off his bike, crossed to her, and wrapped her in a hug. Then he knelt and patted Runeclaw before standing and gesturing at what remained of the building. "Your work?"

Runeclaw replied, "Her fault."

Scarlett bestowed a scowl on the cat, then on Maddox. "Not my work, and not my fault. Jerks, the both of you."

Maddox chuckled. "It looks like something you'd do, though."

Wren came up and hugged Maddox. "Sometimes you lose a battle when you're fighting a war against scumbags. It happens."

Scarlett said, "I'm so sorry I brought them down on you, down on this place."

Wren poked a finger at her face. "We're volunteers, remember? The Witches do what we want, and sometimes there are consequences. The important thing is we got away with only a couple of seriously injured people. That's a success as far as I'm concerned."

Scarlett blinked in surprise. "I thought I saw someone get shot in the head before I left."

"Breanna. She's got a skull made out of rocks. I've always said so."

Lin joined them and added, "And filled with them."

Wren replied, "Doubly defensive."

Everyone laughed, and Lin reported, "She'll be fine. I just checked in. The healing potion handled most of the damage, but she'll need to be watched for a while to be sure. Same with Andrea. Everything looks good."

Scarlett asked, "So now what?"

Maddox grinned and pointed his thumb over his shoulder at the trucks pulling up. "Now you see what a properly motivated magical construction crew can accomplish."

Scarlett watched as he conferred with a number of men who had pulled up in pickup trucks emblazoned with the logo of a construction company.

Lin explained, "We've got experts to tell us what to do, but we'll be the labor today. You'll be impressed."

The man came up to them and nodded. He was clean-cut and wore a button-up blue shirt, khakis, and a hard hat. "First step is demolition and clearing."

Lin grinned. "We're good at that. I'll get some people together. Where do you want the stuff?"

He shrugged. "Wren said you'd deal with the debris later. I got the impression she was thinking of burning it or something."

"Good deal." Lin clapped. "This is the best part." She walked toward a corner of the building where part of the wall still stood. She cast force shields around it on both sides, then threaded power through the remaining gap and slammed force magic into it until the wood splintered and broke. She repeated the process until the whole section had broken away.

When Lin released the shield, Scarlett levitated the junk over into a pile. The drow laughed. "You're a natural."

Runeclaw observed, "Definitely has a rare talent for breaking things."

Scarlett countered, "Why don't you make yourself useful and entertain someone else with that keen wit? We have no need for sarcastic comments at the moment. You're out of luck." She ignored his reply as she turned back to the building. "My turn." She cast her force walls, then used force magic to break up the wall in between them. When it was rubble, they moved it out of the way.

Other Witches were working on different parts of the building, and a group of five collaborated to take care of the roof. That process seemed more difficult since it involved breaking off sections while not causing everything to crash down at once. They carefully used focused lightning to cut through beams and free up pieces to pull down.

As they continued to watch, Scarlett asked, "You've done this before?"

Lin replied, "Yeah. We do this to make money sometimes. Help out a construction crew or whatever. We haven't had to do any major renovations on any of our places, so we haven't had to do it before on our behalf. Pretty sure the Spell Riders did when they converted the garage, though. Not take down the building but break out all the interior stuff that had been there before."

It took until lunchtime to completely clear the place. When they finished, the concrete pad that made up the foundation was visible with nothing attached to it. The experts had tied off or removed the plumbing, electrical, and other utility connections while the Witches and Spell Riders did the heavy work.

Pizzas and sodas appeared as if by magic in the hands of a bunch of Spell Riders who came through a portal, and everyone ate as they looked over the blueprints. They had the original designs, and no one had seen a need to change them. The goal for the day was to frame the structure and hopefully get the walls and the roof in place.

Scarlett thought that was amazingly ambitious, but she knew less about construction than she did about most things, and as Runeclaw would doubtless observe, she didn't know that much about most things.

The process of framing with magic was interesting. The workers told them where beams needed to be placed, and the Witches worked together to levitate them into position. Other Witches helped to build scaffolding or magical platforms for the workers to stand on. In this way, the only time limitation was how quickly the workers could drive in bolts, screws, and nails.

The crew must have worked through the night to figure out exactly what wood was needed, choose good pieces, and cut most of it to the right length because there was little need to do anything except move pieces into place and secure them.

By the time twilight was falling, they had framed the entire structure. They'd hoped to get the walls and roof covered, but the workers had come prepared. Working with the Witches, they rigged tarps to cover everything so overnight rain or morning dew would do nothing to harm the lumber that was already in place.

Rather than go to the warehouse, the Witches and the Spell Riders went into the new Wheels tavern. They portaled in lawn chairs from the Spell Riders' backyard with several grills and some food. A couple of kegs were procured, as well as a bunch of soda and ice, and everyone settled down to drink, talk, and eat.

Scarlett wound up sitting with Amber and Lin while Runeclaw made his way around the room and greeted everyone, accepting the pats that were his due. Scarlett asked, "No one's worried about another attack?"

Amber replied, "We've got complete drone coverage going on. I borrowed some heavy ones from Diana Sheen's people. No one can sneak up on us. If they come here, we'll leave the place to them and go to the warehouse. Then I can use the drones to blast them if needed. If they go to the warehouse, we've already moved the most important stuff to a third location so we can melt away from there as well."

Scarlett shook her head. "I hate those guys."

Lin laughed. "We all hate those guys. You don't have any particular edge there."

Amber asked, "Why do you think they attacked?"

Lin replied, "Because we've been taking them on time and again? Not something they're likely to appreciate."

Scarlett nodded. "I have to say it's probably that, yeah."

Amber countered, "They could have let it go. I mean, they're not aware that we have a line on them with Trane, so as far as they knew, our interactions were done. Even Steven. Done and done."

Scarlett shook her head. "Revenge can be a powerful motivation, I suppose."

Lin ventured, "Or they're still working on their plan and want us out of the way so we can't interfere again."

Scarlett scowled. "Well, all they did is make us mad. I kind of hope Trane doesn't go anywhere before his thing wears off so we can pull him in and beat him."

Lin asked, "For information?"

"That too."

The other woman raised her bottle in a toast. "Well, since revenge is a powerful motivator, here's to getting our revenge on the Veil for breaking our bar."

Scarlett and Amber clinked bottles. Scarlett added, "And soon."

CHAPTER FIFTEEN

After a good night's sleep inspired by the day's effort, which was tiring although they'd used magic instead of muscle for the most part, Scarlett got a call from Amber and portaled to the warehouse. She and Runeclaw located the infomancer up in her office in front of her screens, as usual. When they walked in, Amber rose. "We've been invited to Diana Sheen's place."

Runeclaw jumped onto the desk and flicked his tail in a sign of happiness. Scarlett asked, "What's going on?"

"They've got something to show us."

"Well, let's go then." They portaled into the receiving room at the agents' base. The door opened immediately to reveal a grinning Cara and an even more widely grinning purple-haired troll.

Rath called, "You're it," and ran away. Runeclaw scampered after him. Amber looked toward them, then back at Scarlett. "I take it this isn't a surprise?"

She shook her head. "Those two are like fire and oil. Or maybe fire and more fire. I don't know. They're trouble."

Cara laughed. "That's all accurate. Come on." She took them to a part of the base Scarlett hadn't been in before, a high-tech-looking laboratory with stuff she recognized as medical equipment hanging on the walls.

Kayleigh, the team's technician, was in there. Her blonde hair was spiky, and she wore a white lab coat that looked like it'd seen a lot of use, with the arms rolled up to her elbows.

Amber asked, "So, what's the surprise?"

The tech replied, "After we got notified your place was hit and you didn't know how they'd located it, we thought we'd look at the two captives you gave us most recently." She gestured at a window in the side of the room, and Scarlett followed the move to see one of the captives in a cylindrical tube. Kayleigh hit a button, and a light moved up and down the tube. "Look what we found."

Amber stared at it. "Is that a medical tracker in his leg?"

"Got it in one."

Scarlett frowned. "Wait. We located them with a medical tracker, and they found us with one? Seems pretty coincidental."

Kayleigh replied, "It would have, except the other guy's got one too. The people they deployed against you when you grabbed these two were all sabotaged, for lack of a better word."

Scarlett growled, "Those bastards."

Amber shook her head. "Pretty clever."

Cara interjected, "Nothing like having your ideas turned back against you to make you feel stupid, is there?"

Amber replied, "Scarlett's used to feeling stupid."

She pointed at the infomancer. "Just because Runeclaw's busy doesn't mean you have to stand in for him." Everyone chuckled, and Scarlett added, "Well, that's one mystery solved, anyway."

Cara continued. "Wren mentioned you've got a surveillance problem. Want to share?"

Amber explained, "We've got a tracer on a member of the Veil, Kingston Trane. But it's wearing off, so we'll lose it in a couple of days. Maybe three or four, tops."

"Surveillance is something we're pretty good at. Kayleigh, any recommendations?"

The technician scratched the back of her neck. "What's his house like?"

Scarlett replied, "Big house in the front, trees on the other three sides, although a pretty solid distance away from the house. There was a lot of empty ground to sneak through to get inside."

Cara asked, "You can't do that again?"

Scarlett shrugged. "We could, but we got lucky the first time. Doing it again would be pretty risky."

Amber explained, "That's one of our backup plans. Along with bringing him in and beating on him for a while."

Kayleigh asked, "What's the security like?"

Amber replied, "Motion sensors, sound sensors, thermal, magic. The usual things."

Kayleigh grinned. "All right. I'm pretty sure I've got the solution for you. Come to my lab."

They encountered Rath and Runeclaw dashing through the hallways as they went. Neither looked tired or bored with their ongoing game of chase. Scarlett yelled, "Don't break anything. We can't afford to fix it."

Cara laughed. "Rath breaks stuff all the time. He is completely unapologetic. The fact that he can turn into a seven-foot monster version of himself kind of makes us let it slide."

Amber asked, "Can you imagine if Runeclaw could become the size of a giant panther?"

Scarlett rubbed her forehead. "The very idea gives me a headache. Let's never think about that again."

When they arrived in the lab, which had several worktables and displays scattered around, Kayleigh pulled a small briefcase off a shelf. She set it on a worktable and opened it to show several bricks, each about the size of Scarlett's clenched fist. "These have a bunch of good features for audio surveillance, using a different approach than most similar equipment uses.

"Each of these does its sensing and shoots up the data to a satellite every few milliseconds in a randomized pattern so there's no way to sense it being transmitted. It's a constant trickle of data that pattern analyzers won't catch. A computer puts all that information back together into actual sound."

Amber replied, "Nice. Sneaky."

Kayleigh grinned. "Sneaky is always useful. You'll notice the boxes match the color of the insert in the case. They use adaptive camouflage skins to match whatever you put them against. Each one has an internal battery that'll be good for several days. They can do a little solar charging through the adaptive skin, but that will only extend their life a tiny bit. They're not optimized for it, so don't count on it."

Amber nodded as if she understood.

Scarlett didn't. "Then what?"

Kayleigh grinned again. "Then you'll have ears on the inside. The software's sophisticated and will be able to figure out what's coming from where, separate all the frequencies so we know which are from different sources, and generally give you a perfect audio picture of what's going on inside."

Amber asked, "Does it do video?"

"Nope. Sound only. We have a video version, but it's bigger, more obvious, and works for a shorter duration before needing to be recharged. But we'll position a high-altitude surveillance drone nearby for you. If there's something to see outside, we'll spot it for you."

Scarlett took the box after Kayleigh closed it. "This is amazing. Thank you."

Kayleigh nodded. "Don't mention it. Just call when you're ready to put the pieces into position so we can assist you in placing them."

Amber asked, "Do you have a tracer of any kind that we can use on Trane?"

"Tons. But planting them would be the same challenge as renewing your marker, and they'd probably be more easily noticed."

"I figured, but I thought I'd ask."

Cara asked, "Anything else?"

Scarlett rolled her eyes. "Help me separate Runeclaw from Rath."

The other woman laughed. "Easier said than done."

Later that day, Scarlett portaled into the tree line near Kingston Trane's house. She crouched there for several minutes while Amber used the enhanced sensor pack she wore to look for any changes to the defensive arrangement since her last visit. Scarlett's stress level increased by the second as she waited for the infomancer to speak until Amber finally advised, "We're all good. Kayleigh?"

The tech replied, "All right. If you're currently facing twelve o'clock, we'll go with one just off to your right, one at about one o'clock, and one over there in the far tree line at about nine o'clock. That'll give us a good solid triangulation on the house."

"On the move." Scarlett stayed under a veil as she made her way through the trees. The first one was easy. Getting to the second one required pausing while a security patrol went by but wasn't otherwise challenging.

The third proved the most difficult because a security patrol was taking a break right in front of it. Scarlett waited as the seconds ticked by and they chatted about inane things. She muttered, "If there were no magic sensors, I'd create phantom dogs to chase them away."

Laughs came over the comm. Kayleigh offered, "I could crash the drone on them."

"A little obvious."

"Oh, but phantom dogs aren't obvious at all."

Finally, the guards left, and Scarlett placed the third box.

Kayleigh reported, "I've got the signals. Stand by. They're feeding the satellite properly. All right, greens across the board. It'll take the computers a couple of hours to get everything filtered and processed, but then you'll be able to listen in real-time."

Amber replied, "Thanks so much."

Kayleigh's grin was audible over the comm. "Any time. This is what we do."

CHAPTER SIXTEEN

The next day, Scarlett got to the warehouse early in anticipation of listening to Trane's house and whatever secrets he might have to share. She brought coffee to the infomancer, and together they watched the video feed Kayleigh was providing, which showed nothing of interest. They listened to the goings-on in the house, which were even less engaging.

After ten minutes, Runeclaw flopped down on his side on Amber's desk, stretched his front and back paws as far as they would go, and muttered, "Boring. Nap time."

Scarlett replied, "You've only been up for an hour."

"Someone has to take the night shift guarding us."

Scarlett snorted. "Yeah, and it's not you. News flash, buddy, you snore." She'd heard someone use that phrase and thought it was funny once someone explained what a news flash was.

Runeclaw ignored her, and Amber reached out to pet the cat. "Don't be mean to my kitty friend."

"You want him?"

Amber looked over her shoulder and shook her head emphatically but replied, "Of course I do. He's adorable."

Scarlett laughed. They chatted as they waited for something to occur. Finally, things started to get interesting when Kingston Trane started berating his servants. It sounded like normal inquiries from them about what he'd like for breakfast and what he'd like to wear, but they were all responded to with snappish anger. Scarlett observed, "Our friend seems a little edgy today."

Amber replied, "Let's hope it's for good reason."

The next hour was equally dull, but then the phone rang. Kayleigh had also provided another display that offered a schematic of Trane's house along with an indication of where the sound was coming from, and it showed the only phone ringing was in his office, suggesting it was a special line.

He picked it up instantly. "Yes?" There was no trace of the irritability in his tone.

The audio surveillance perfectly replicated the other side of the phone call, impressing Scarlett. A man instructed, "You'll need to be here tomorrow night at seven PM."

"Excellent. Will I have to be responsible for anything upon arrival?"

"Only to make yourself available if something is needed. The gathering itself starts at eight."

Trane sounded excited. "Very good. Excellent. Everything is as it should be, despite the—" He paused and said in an even more hushed tone, "Setbacks?"

The man's tone was confident. "It is."

Trane repeated, "Excellent."

"Any questions?"

"None."

The line dropped without any farewells, and Trane called for his personnel. He instructed, "I will need my tuxedo ready for tomorrow night."

A man's cultured voice replied, "Very good, sir. And your robes?"

"Not necessary. This is a mixed affair, so only the tuxedo. I will, of course, carry my wand and be accompanied by my security. They must also be appropriately attired."

"Of course, sir."

Scarlett met Amber's gaze. "That sounds like something interesting."

The other woman nodded. "It definitely does."

"Finally. Let's see what else we can find out before we call everyone together."

They listened for the rest of the day and picked up other tidbits of information. It all pointed to an important event happening the following evening at a location that wasn't spoken aloud. When Trane went to sleep earlier than usual, Amber set her computers to record and they portaled to Wheels.

The inside had been fully framed and drywalled, electricity and plumbing were functioning, and a single table had been brought in along with some chairs. Scarlett recognized the furniture from the backyard of the Spell Riders' garage.

Maddox and Snow were already there, and Lin called a greeting as Scarlett, Runeclaw, and Amber headed for the table. They grabbed some pizza from the boxes on top of it, then accepted bottles of beer from Snow, drawn from a cooler on the floor beside him.

Wren arrived too. "All right. We've listened to the stuff you sent over. Clearly, there's something going on."

Scarlett replied, "This has to be what they've been working toward, whatever it is."

Snow supplied, "A gathering."

Scarlett rolled her eyes. "Yeah, I think we all figured that out by the way he specifically said, 'the gathering.'"

Maddox interjected, "Snow is very smart. He likes to prove it from time to time."

Runeclaw observed, "He should work harder."

Lin remarked, "Trane called it a mixed crowd. That suggests it's not a magical ritual like the collaring was."

Amber added, "He's also going to be wearing a tux. That means it's some kind of formal event."

Maddox replied, "Whatever it is, I think we can assume it involves the collars, will be heavily guarded, and it's a party we need to crash."

There was general agreement around the table. Wren asked, "Which brings us to the next problem. How do we accomplish that?"

Amber reminded them, "The trace is still good for another few days. The audio surveillance will let us know when Trane leaves, and the trace should tell us where he goes."

Wren asked, "Are the Riders with us on this one?"

Maddox and Snow both nodded, and the former added, "Hell yeah, we are. It's your show, but we'll play whatever role you need us to."

"We'll have everyone organized into teams, and as soon

as we know where they're going, we'll get nearby. We should be able to fall on the place like an avalanche as long as it's not a fortified bunker or something."

Scarlett observed, "Risky going in blind. I think I have an idea to help with that, though."

Snow smiled. "I bet I know what you're thinking."

Scarlett nodded. "You do. The magic and technology hybrid holographic disguises we used before. We could use those again. Could you do up another set?"

"I'll lose a little sleep, but not a problem to have it ready by tomorrow afternoon."

"Perfect. Lin and I can go in, take a look around, and figure out what's going on. And most importantly, identify which Robes are present so we can take them out as soon as things get noisy. Taking them off the board early has to be worth the effort."

Wren replied, "As long as you don't start your action until we're ready to go. That way, if it blows up, we can move immediately rather than giving them time to react."

"Sounds good." They talked tactics for a while longer, then Wren, Maddox, and Snow ambled off to their tasks.

Lin remarked, "Just so I understand this, the plan is for us to intercept someone headed for the party and replace them?"

Scarlett replied, "Yeah, that's the gist of it."

"That's kind of out there, even for you."

"I know. It's even worse than most of my ideas since Runeclaw will have to stay with the assault team."

The cat had remained mostly silent during the previous discussion but spoke up now. "I hate this plan."

Scarlett reached out and scratched behind his ears. "I

know, buddy. But it's unlikely whoever we detain will be bringing a cat. Plus, since the Veil knows you and I are partners, even if they were bringing a cat to the formal event, it would be risky for us to copy that."

"I could sneak in."

"True, and Wren might have you do that. But I don't see any way you can help us with our part of it."

He blinked slowly as if considering his options. "All right. But you save some bad guys for me."

Scarlett laughed. "Count on it."

CHAPTER SEVENTEEN

Camus put his pen in its holder and gestured for Ellis to take the seat across from him. As the other man did so, Camus asked, "Are things progressing as expected?"

"They are."

"Give me a rundown of the security, please." Camus had little doubt it was under control but needed the reassurance, nonetheless.

Ellis closed his eyes as if checking a mental list, then opened them again. "The guests will arrive either by limo or on a designated portal space outside. They'll be escorted by security personnel dressed as valets and footmen. That's the first line of the internal defense since our infomancers will use their glasses to scan the new arrivals."

Camus leaned back and steepled his fingers. "Good. Next?"

"The security process from there is pretty standard. They will pass through a sensor station that can identify metal, magic, and explosives."

"The first two will go off for everybody, probably. We

can expect all the normal subtle illusions and small magics that always occur at functions like these."

Ellis nodded. "We'll have a magical there to help us make the assessments if anyone warrants a closer look. We'll also have a team on hand to give a more targeted scan if needed."

Camus frowned as he considered the implications. "Do your best, but do not irritate the guests. We need them in a buying mood."

"Understood. Gold Robe will arrive at seven to be on hand if any last-minute details need to be handled. The collared servants are all ready to go. They'll be getting final instructions and checks today before the event."

"You'll need to collect the ones from the Robes who are no longer with us."

Ellis offered a thin smile. "That's already underway."

Camus nodded in approval. "It sounds like everything is well-handled. I would have expected nothing less. I will be spending most of the day in my room downstairs. Please be available to escort me upstairs ten minutes before the event begins."

Ellis stood, recognizing the dismissal. "Of course."

That evening at five minutes until seven, Amber notified everyone about Trane being on the move. He portaled from one spot to the next for five minutes, but at seven precisely, he stopped bouncing around. A search was undertaken to find the Witch or Rider with the nearest portal, and a Witch was dispatched to get close to the target location.

The estimate was that she would arrive around eight, so at seven-thirty, Scarlett and Lin were in the locker area in the warehouse, preparing for the evening's adventure.

Lin asked, "So, you're pretty sure these disguises will work, hmmm?"

Scarlett nodded. "They worked fine before. Shouldn't be a problem. It works on some kind of pulse detection, defeats the sensor, I don't know. Even if they trigger an anti-magic emitter, the tech should kick in and keep the disguise going."

"So, we'll have to generate the disguise magically with illusion, but the technology will match it?"

"You got it."

Lin grinned. "In that case, I'm gonna bring a lot of guns."

Scarlett laughed. "We've been over this. You can't bring a lot of guns."

The other woman pouted. "Why not?"

"It's a dinner party. Visual disguise won't do anything if someone bumps into you and feels a rifle across your chest."

Lin shook her head, looking disappointed. "You are a spoilsport."

Scarlett laughed. "Whatever. The goal here is subtlety. I know that's not something you're entirely comfortable with, but I'm sure you can manage it if you try hard enough."

"Rude."

Scarlett turned to her locker full of gear. She had the same problem. Most of the things she would normally carry, like the knives in their back sheaths or the revolver at the small of her back, would be too easily noticed. She didn't expect a pat down or anything similarly personal, but it was a possibility they couldn't ignore. Thus, they needed to be as much like what the illusion showed them to be as possible.

She added, "Also, no body armor."

Lin scowled and put the vest she'd been pulling out of her locker back in. "Habit."

Amber's conversation in her ear with the Witch who was heading to Trane's location on her motorcycle stole Scarlett's attention for a time. Then she sorted through her stuff again and finally decided all she could bring would be Fang, her wand, and her bandolier of darts. The darts would need to go under her clothes, and she'd have to reach under her shirt to get at them. Fang would be in a sheath around her calf, and her wand would be up her sleeve, as usual.

She donned the items, stood, and practiced reaching down for Fang and under her shirt to retrieve the darts.

Lin watched her and snickered. "This is a pathetic way to go into a fight."

Scarlett made a face at the other woman. "We'll be behind enemy lines. We need cleverness and brains, not weapons."

"Yeah, yeah." Lin didn't need a wand to perform her magic, which Scarlett envied. For the drow, leaving behind pistols, rifles, and other implements of deadly force was not something done lightly. Lin pulled a purse out from the cabinet and loaded it with items Scarlett hadn't seen before.

Scarlett asked, "Is that makeup?"

Lin stuck her tongue out at Scarlett. "I do wear it sometimes, you know."

"Yeah, but I've never seen you carry it into combat."

The other woman chuckled. "Fair. The lipsticks are smoke grenades. The rest of the stuff is flash-bangs. Nothing explosive that can be detected by any standard sensors, so no need to worry about that."

Scarlett was impressed. "Where did you get that?"

"You're not the only one who knows fancy people. I have a friend who works for the government and does this kind of concealing work and building detection for it. She gave me some prototypes a while back. I haven't had any call to use them because, you know, I normally carry actual grenades."

"Handy. Very handy." She paused, expecting that Runeclaw would add something insulting to the conversation, then remembered he was with Wren. She shook her head and grumbled, "I'm gonna miss Runeclaw during this."

Lin chuckled. "Don't worry. I'm sure he won't be far away and will cause trouble galore."

Scarlett stood. "All right then. Let's go grab the other physical disguises and head out to the portal, shall we?"

Camus opened his eyes slowly as the portion of his mind he'd set to track the passing of time warned him that he needed to get moving. He had changed into his tuxedo immediately upon entering his sanctuary and had used magic to clear off his ritual circle so he wouldn't get even a grain of dust on the pristine fabric.

He rose with a grunt at the stiffness that had built up in his muscles, banished the protective rings, and moved to his cabinet. He would love to be able to bring his battle staff to show these people who he truly was, but tonight he was playing a role. The people invited to the gathering believed him to be an eccentric and wealthy man who dabbled in things no one else would.

To that end, he had procured artifacts for them, had things stolen on their behalf, and had loaned and donated money to various enterprises to build their relationship, all with an eye toward this moment. Many people of lesser power already possessed one of his collared servants.

They would be useful, but he had left the most powerful people he hoped to entice with a collared servant for last. He'd known word would get to them and had counted on it. It was finally time to see what kind of result their plans had brought into being.

He tapped his pocket to ensure his healing potion was in place and slid his wand into the other one. People sometimes shook hands and gripped forearms, and he didn't want them grabbing his wand. Fortunately, this group wasn't made up of huggers, so he could keep it fairly well hidden. He checked his look in the mirror, adjusted his bow tie, and spoke the words that would bring the door out of the room back into existence.

When he stepped outside, Ellis was waiting as he'd expected. The man had changed into his tuxedo, less fine than Camus' but still appropriate, and gestured toward the stairs. "All is in readiness, sir."

"Gold Robe?"

"Awaiting us one level up. He wants to walk in at your side."

Camus let out something that was half chuckle and half snort. "Of course he does. Well, that's fine. He can come in a step behind, anyway."

"I'll ensure he does."

When they reached the top level, Gold Robe fell in line behind them without a word. Camus was sure his expression had silenced the other man. He felt intense. Focused. Ready to seal the deal and send some of these rich and powerful people home with a servant they would believe they could control. They would be able to, right up until the moment he asserted his control and used it to capture those who thought they were in charge.

As they neared the room, Ellis advised, "The first guests have passed through security and are waiting in the foyer."

Camus forced a smile onto his lips. The Veil's future was at hand. All he had to do was be nothing short of stellar. There was not even a single sliver of doubt in his mind that he would accomplish his goal. "Well, all right then. Let's go meet our customers."

CHAPTER EIGHTEEN

Amber's voice sounded in Scarlett's ear as she walked toward the open portal. "I've got a drone way up high so nobody notices. This place is immense, at least twice as big as Trane's place. One of multiple entrances on the right-hand side of the building is lit up.

"Several limos are already parked in an area off to the side, far enough from the house that they wouldn't damage it even if they exploded. Thermal imaging shows a ring of bodies around the house in a more or less symmetrical arrangement, grouped by threes."

Wren asked, "Simple security or soldiers?"

Amber replied, "Can't tell from this distance, sorry. But the arrangement makes it seem like they know what they're doing."

"It's fine. We'll be there soon enough." Wren sounded half tense and half excited. The tone was familiar from other operations and meant the other woman was firmly in the zone of command, hyper-focused on strategy, tactics, and the protection of those under her care.

Another Witch joined Scarlett and Lin as they stepped through the portal. The trio moved swiftly across the lower part of the lawn toward where the limos were turning in from the main road. They crouched among the greenery and watched several roll past. The oncoming line was visible from the drone's view in her glasses.

Scarlett murmured, "That one in the back. Think we might have a little time after it."

Their temporary partner, Emma, replied, "I'll step out in the road and stop it so you two can do your thing."

Lin reminded her, "Shield yourself in case they don't stop fast enough."

The other woman grinned. "Not my first time."

"Yeah, and I don't want it to be your last."

Scarlett ordered, "Go." Emma stepped in front of the limo, waving her hands to catch the driver's attention. The one that had passed didn't react, thankfully, but the one they were targeting stopped. Emma moved around toward the driver as Scarlett hustled around the back toward the far rear door while Lin took the nearer one. The driver rolled down his window to talk, and Emma did something, probably telekinetically, to unlock the doors.

Scarlett and Lin ripped them open, and all three used magical lightning to knock out the car's occupants. A moment later, after throwing up a veil to hide their actions, they opened a portal and threw all three occupants through it to waiting hands on the far side in the warehouse.

Scarlett instructed, "Give us their wallets." The man's wallet floated to her, and the woman's purse flew to Lin.

Scarlett laughed. "Looks like I get to be the bigwig and you're the lackey."

"Lame."

The people on the other side handed across the finishing pieces of their disguises. Scarlett shrugged on the tuxedo shirt and jacket while Lin wriggled into a dress. They both kept their shiny shoes, which were unisex enough to pass.

Then they climbed into the back of the limo, and Lin instructed, "Oh, driver, let's go."

Emma, who had also put on a disguise appropriate for the limo driver, replied in a fake British accent, "Right you are. Away we go. Chop-chop, yo-ho, and all that."

Lin growled, "We are not pirates."

Emma laughed.

Scarlett opened the wallet and spoke the name on the license. Immediately, data flowed onto the clear-lensed glasses she wore to tell her about her target. Unfortunately, he didn't wear glasses, so she wouldn't be able to keep them. She concentrated on digesting as much information as possible while they drove up the hill, and Lin did the same thing with her subject.

Before they reached the top, Scarlett spoke the word to activate her holographic disguise and cast the spell to match it. Lin did her own a moment later.

When the car stopped, the doors were opened immediately by a pair of men in dark sunglasses, which was a strange look for the evening.

She ignored the offered hand, stepped out, and buttoned her jacket in a way she'd seen men do countless times. Lin accepted the assistance on her side as Scarlett walked around. Scarlett offered a word of thanks to the man, then gestured for Lin to precede her.

The footman closed the doors and waved for the car to move on.

Lin muttered, "Facial recognition?"

"Can't think of another reason for the glasses unless they're scanning the cars for explosives."

"Could be. Not a bad idea."

Scarlett observed, "I guess that depends on how exciting their parties usually are." Lin laughed, and they stepped into line behind several others waiting to clear security. They passed through the sensor without setting off any alarms, and while a guard took a cursory look into Lin's bag, no further examination occurred. As they moved over to get a drink, Scarlett asked, "Why limos? Why not portal?"

Lin chuckled. "Sometimes showing how rich you are involves doing things the most ostentatious way, rather than the most efficient one."

Scarlett sipped her champagne. "Seems silly."

Wren asked via comms, "What do you see?"

Pretending to talk to Lin, Scarlett pointed out the room's features. "The staircase curves up to the second level. It's lovely. Looks like marble. I'm guessing there are rooms to either side of this one, probably smaller ones, but those double doors opposite the entrance look like they lead to something. Maybe there will be dancing or a full dinner."

Lin snorted. "If it's dancing, I'm leaving. Dinner, I'm in."

Scarlett raised an eyebrow and wondered how it looked

in her disguise. Her target had been a relatively portly man, bigger and taller than she was. Lin's was not too far from the drow's normal look but with longer hair and a bonier body type. "I think I see cameras up there. I wonder if they're recording what we're saying. If so, you might have offended our host if he likes dancing."

Lin made a kissy face toward them and smacked her lips. "Well, if so, I hope they're getting my good side."

"All your sides are good sides, darling," Scarlett replied absently. She touched her wand and whispered a spell that would hopefully mess with microphones that were doubtless listening to them. "I don't see anyone with the unique neckwear we expected to see."

"Must be coming a little later."

"Unless this is something else entirely and we're wasting our time."

Amber interjected, "I've been doing facial recognition on the other people in the room. These are power players. We've got politicians, CEOs, media executives, and so on. Whatever's going on here, it's bound to be serious."

Lin gasped and stiffened. Scarlett followed her gaze to see the man she'd last seen wearing crimson robes. He was trailed by Kingston Trane and accompanied by a hard-looking man in a tux who was Crimson's security.

Scarlett commented brightly, "Ah, our host approaches. Relax, sweetheart, he's just a guy. An impressive one, sure, but just a guy like any other."

Lin managed a laugh. "Yeah, that. He's important, though."

Scarlett put a bit of steel into her voice. "Yes, there are important people here, but you only have to worry about one. Me." She caught an approving glance from a nearby man who seemed to like that she'd put her apparent subordinate in her place.

Lin replied, "Well, we're about to have a meeting of the important ones, then."

Scarlett looked up. The man was walking toward her. She set her glass aside and stepped forward with a smile. Their hands met in the middle, and she shook his vigorously. He spoke first, saying, "Robert, so glad you could make it. Wouldn't have been the same without you. It's lovely to finally shake your hand."

She smiled, thankful this pair hadn't met in person. "And yours. Thank you for the invitation. Your house is lovely."

He looked around it with a smile. "It serves its purpose. As for thanking me, well, thank me after you see the wonderful gift that awaits you."

Scarlett laughed. "Care to share a hint?"

He laughed too, but it sounded louder and more forced than it needed to be. "You'll have to wait your turn like all the others. Don't worry, though. There's plenty to go around."

He moved on to engage the next nearest guest. Scarlett shook her head. When he was far enough away not to hear, she remarked, "That's a man who's good with people. I could never be that engaging."

Lin replied, "I'm sure this is where your partner would agree, although I think you do pretty well. But what the hell does he mean by wonderful gift?"

"I can think of only one thing."

Crimson clapped, and the room fell silent and turned

toward him. He stood by the double doors, and at a gesture, they opened to display a ballroom beyond. "If you all come right this way, we'll get things started."

The crowd moved toward the opening, and as she and Lin fell in line, Scarlett murmured, "I guess we're about to find out what presents await us all."

CHAPTER NINETEEN

Scarlett moved immediately off to the side after crossing the threshold into the ballroom. The space was enormous. The floor was polished parquet intended for dancing, although it might work for a basketball game, given the size of the space.

She imagined the dance floor would easily handle more than a hundred people with room left over all around for mingling. The guests tonight didn't reach that number, which allowed her to keep an eye on them as they wandered in.

Most of the attendees were men, accompanied by an even split of male and female assistants or partners. Their subordinate status in the relationship was obvious. The women who were among the powerful uniformly had men at their side. Scarlett muttered, "Odd bunch."

Lin replied, "Odd room."

Scarlett's gaze traveled across the walls, noting the large blackout curtains set at regular intervals. Only the slightest bit of light leakage indicated the windows behind them.

That light must have come from the exterior grounds. She had noticed they were well-illuminated, doubtless to keep anyone wishing the household occupants harm from getting close unseen.

Scarlett scanned the room's far end to the corner. She stiffened, forced herself to relax, and muttered, "Bastards."

Lin replied in a voice that held restrained anger, "More of them here than I thought there would be."

"Me too."

The collared captives stood in several ranks on a raised platform that was probably a stage when the room served its nominal purpose. Three rows each held ten figures standing more or less at attention.

Scarlett looked from them to the people arrayed around the room and realized the numbers lined up with a couple of collared captives to spare. Some looked scared, which made sense, while others seemed resigned. She muttered, "I wonder where they got the others from."

Lin replied, "We better get moving, or someone will notice."

Scarlett took a halting step, then shoved herself back into her role and confidently marched across the room. Crimson stood at the far end, where a semicircle was forming around him with the principals on the inside and their assistants or partners behind them. Scarlett took her place among them, crossed her arms, and waited.

Almost uniformly, the group avoided one another's eyes. She wasn't sure if that was a normal practice among people of this status to prevent an inadvertent challenge to another or if they were ashamed of what had brought them here. She hoped the latter was true for some.

Crimson began, "I am Camus, as you all know. I have brought you here because you are the leaders. The principals. The forward thinkers, those who see an opportunity, grab onto it, and never let go. You are the people who make our country work. Hell, you're the people who make the *world* work."

There was some polite laughter and nods in response. "As such, you deserve some luxuries others don't have access to. What I have to offer is exclusive, with no other source but me."

He flashed a smile. "Don't worry. I'm not gouging you on price and all that."

The group laughed. He was striking the exact proper notes of confidence and obsequiousness that said he knew he wasn't one of them, but he still had something valuable to offer they could get nowhere else. Scarlett joined in the appreciative amusement to maintain her cover.

Camus continued. "The people you see before you have volunteered for this. They wish to be part of your businesses and households. I've described it as the most exclusive internship ever."

He gestured at the collars. "These devices allow you some control over their actions. Most importantly, they prevent these potential assets from speaking about your activities. They physically cannot betray you."

There were some murmurs at that.

"You who deal in the world of corporate secrets on a day-to-day level need something like this, I know, which is why I've provided it. They will take other commands as well, but nothing that fundamentally conflicts with their principles."

He pointed at one of the men in the group. "Sorry, Steve, you can't send one to kill your friend Lance, there."

They laughed.

Steve said, "Damn."

Lance replied, "I'll sleep better tonight knowing that."

Scarlett immediately disliked both men. Most of the group hit her senses that way. The avaricious looks in their eyes made her want to smack them. With a fist. Made of force. The size of a door.

She was pulled back from her fantasy vision of doing that by Camus saying, "We can discuss price after you've established your interest. I encourage you to talk to them. Find out which one would suit you best. We have plenty of time."

Scarlett nodded for Lin to accompany her, then intercepted one of the captives as they left the platform and moved to circulate through the room. The girl was college-age, as they all were, a brunette who looked less scared than resigned. "So, what kinds of things can you do for me?"

The girl shrugged. "Everything from laundry to guarding your most valuable secrets, sir."

"And you literally can't speak the secrets to anyone else."

She laughed. It was a dark, unhappy sound. A hand tapped her collar. "This won't allow it. It's magic."

Scarlett frowned. "Wouldn't anti-magic emitters solve that?"

The girl shrugged. "You'd have to ask someone smarter than me about that, but we were told to stay away from them."

Another executive wandered over to speak to the girl. Scarlett and Lin backed away, out of the press.

Lin murmured, "That sounds ominous."

Scarlett nodded. "It does. We'll have to mention that to Snow."

Lin's lips twitched with the effort of holding back the frown Scarlett knew was trying to break out. "Look at all these mighty people. They're going to do it. They're going to take these captives home."

Scarlett shook her head. "Camus chose his audience well." She raised a hand to cover her mouth and faked a cough. "Be sure to break out thumbscrews for the scumbag I'm pretending to be."

Wren replied, "Will do. We're in position and will go if something breaks out here or when you give the word."

"I don't think we can wait much longer, but let's give these people as much time as possible to show their true selves."

A small commotion near the exit caught her attention. Two executives were leaving, visibly upset.

She mentioned it, and a moment later, Amber replied, "I've got them. They're heading for their limos." Several minutes later, Amber reported, "Vans pulled up in front of and behind them. They're pulling everyone out of the limos and loading them into the vans."

Wren replied, "All right, that tears it. The Spell Riders will rescue those people. Time for us to do our jobs. We're coming in."

CHAPTER TWENTY

Runeclaw stood behind Wren and braced himself for her next words. She informed everyone, "All right. We're going with the base plan. Simultaneous attack from all sides. Spell Riders, maintain the outer perimeter and catch anyone who tries to get past you."

Maddox replied, "We're on it. The people from the limos and the vans are all under control, and the road is clear."

"Good." Wren grinned at Runeclaw. "Let's cause some trouble, kitty cat. Witches, go, go, go."

Runeclaw surged forward as Wren did the same beside him. His senses had already picked out the nearest guards, and they reacted quickly as the first sound of a falling guard reached their ears. The veils the Witches had cast were excellent, but it was inevitable that someone would fall outside them and make a sound.

A gun came up pointed at Wren, and she dove to the ground. Runeclaw kept running forward, leapt to the man's vest, dug in his claws, and launched into his face. Runeclaw touched his tail to the man's temple and discharged lightning. His foe stuttered and shook for a moment, then his eyes rolled back in his head, and he collapsed.

Runeclaw jumped free. He had no time to waste but needed to ensure each man he took down stayed down. This necessitated close-contact blasts rather than wide, sweeping ones. The constant gunfire happened above him, and no one looked for a cat in the chaos and confusion. He stayed relatively near Wren but ranged outward to take out other guards when she paused to issue commands or deal with one of her own.

He had taken three of them out of the fight by the time he reached the entrance to the house. A man in an expensive tuxedo was running out with a frantic look, doubtless in reaction to the shouts of alarm from the inside. Runeclaw laughed and blasted everyone nearby with lightning. They all went down fast.

He blasted another security man a moment later, but a magic bubble protected him. Runeclaw dodged to the side as return lightning came from somewhere and scoured the ground where he'd been.

Wren shouted, "We've got magic opposition outside."

Scarlett replied, "We've got it in here, too."

When the security guards had sounded the warning, she and Lin had headed toward the exit from the ballroom and separated any of the guests who were trying to drag out one of the collared captives. With that accomplished, she looked around the room and spotted Kingston Trane running out a side door.

She snapped, "Lin, they're running."

Scarlett and Lin raced for the door Trane had used. When they got past it, they heard a noise from the right and pelted in that direction. Turning a corner, they saw a door at the end of the hallway swinging closed and ran as fast as they could in that direction. Scarlett drew her wand, pumped magic into her muscles, added protection to the shield around her, and dispelled her disguise. Lin did the same.

They were almost at the end of the hallway when immediate gunfire followed the sound of a door opening behind them. Lin shouted a string of curses and fell forward. Scarlett spun and blindly threw a blast of force magic that filled the hallway behind her.

The man who had accompanied Crimson Robe—she still thought of him that way despite now knowing his name—slammed back against the wall. He held onto his pistol until Scarlett shaped another blast of force magic and slammed it into his hand to send the weapon skittering down the corridor.

She stomped forward, drew Fang from its sheath in a smooth movement, and stabbed it into his shoulder. His knees buckled, and he fell. She ran to help Lin, but the other woman was already fishing out a healing potion.

Lin muttered, "It'll be fine. Go. I'll be with you in a minute."

Scarlett ran for the door.

Runeclaw raced into the building, darted through the ballroom, and headed down the hallway. He smelled Scarlett's scent and knew which turns she had taken. When he turned the corner and saw Lin on the floor, he snarled and zapped the fallen man near her with a blast of electricity to make sure he stayed down. He slid to a stop next to Lin.

"I'm fine. Scarlett's downstairs. Go help her." Lin flicked her wrist, and the door at the end of the hall banged open.

Runeclaw hurtled forward and ran down the steps. They opened onto a huge basement, more than a story high and almost as wide as the ballroom had been. It held two wizards who were blasting magic at Scarlett. She was wrapped in a force shield and slowly walked toward them. Runeclaw slipped up beside her and bumped against her leg so she'd know he was there without looking down.

She asked, "Left or right?"

"Left first."

"Go."

Runeclaw dashed off to the left in a wide curve. The wizard didn't track his movements but kept attacking Scarlett. That gave Runeclaw plenty of time to get close, line up, and jump on him. The man screamed as Runeclaw's nails dug into the flesh of his arm, but they didn't penetrate as far as they should have through his shields.

A moment later, Runeclaw flew through the air away from him. *That's not good.* He wrenched his body around to prepare for landing.

Scarlett was surprised to see the man shrug Runeclaw off. It was rare that anyone could defend against a surprise attack from the cat. She shifted her efforts away from Camus despite her desire to take him out and sent a blast of force at the other one.

Trane backpedaled, throwing magic at her and Runeclaw with a growing look of panic. She considered throwing Fang, but it was dark, and she wasn't sure of her throw despite Rath's instruction. She was much better with the knife up close. *So, get close.*

She dashed forward and pushed magic into her shields to deal with the constant barrage of force and shadow magic Trane slammed into them. A distant part of her mind noted that Runeclaw had landed safely and was coming back into the fight, but she intended to make his participation unnecessary. That plan lasted only a moment longer before a piece of the ceiling collapsed on her without warning.

Scarlett barely managed to shift power to her overhead shield in time to protect herself as she was driven to the floor by the weight of the stone. The attack hadn't come from Trane, which meant Camus was still in the fight, the bastard.

She gathered her magic and blasted a wave of force outward. Her magical link with Runeclaw allowed her to create a carveout in his direction so the flying debris wouldn't impact him. Unfortunately, Trane and Camus were similarly unaffected. She snarled a curse as she ignored Camus again and ran toward Trane.

She pulled out Fang and stabbed at him as she reached close range, but at the same moment, a blast of power hit her from behind and propelled her past her target. She slammed into the wall and dropped the dagger from numb fingers as her hand struck.

Trane turned and slashed his wand at her, and she went to the ground just in time to avoid the laser-like blast of flame that carved into the rock over her head. Her shield could probably handle it, but she wasn't sure what she faced at this point. Both men had more power than they should, or maybe they had been hiding it until now. Either way, it was daunting.

Runeclaw made his presence known by jumping onto Trane and clawing up his back. The wizard spun and smashed his back into a pillar, but Runeclaw jumped away before being caught in between. Trane sent a lance of electricity at the cat that Runeclaw dodged as he bolted back into the shadows. Their quick combat gave Scarlett the room she needed to get into position.

She hurled Fang and chased the dagger. The wizard spun and batted Fang away with a burst of force magic, leaving him open with her inside his guard. It was too dangerous to treat him gently since she didn't know what Camus was up to. She punched Trane in the throat.

He staggered backward with a look of complete shock, unable to breathe, but didn't drop his wand. She reached out with her telekinesis, grabbed Fang, and stabbed him in the chest over his heart. He clutched the dagger and fell.

Scarlett dashed after Camus, but he disappeared through an opening in the wall that closed immediately after him. She cursed, then looked at Runeclaw. "Thank you for not following him. I was sure you were going to be stupid."

He looked at her, then laughed. She laughed at him. He retorted, "I'm not the stupid one here. You've used all the stupid. There's none left for anyone else."

She looked down her nose at him. "That's impolite." She examined the wall and cast a couple of spells at it but couldn't get it open. "Let's go upstairs."

Everyone she saw on the main floor was a Witch or Spell Rider. The ballroom was full of people sitting with their hands cuffed behind them. Half of the room contained the executives and their assistants. The other half held people who worked at the mansion and the security that protected it.

Scarlett asked, "Where are the collared people?"

Wren turned from what she was doing. "They're at a private hospital where they can be checked out and kept safe."

"Why not a regular hospital?"

"I think Snow has something in mind, but he won't share it. I trust him. He's only crazy part of the time."

Scarlett laughed darkly. "All right. What's the plan with these idiots?" She gestured at the executives and their helpers. "How can I help?"

Wren sighed. "As much as I would like to beat on them for a while—and believe me, I would *really* like to beat on them for a while—we're going to let them go. We have no jurisdiction here. What we *do* have is their identification and the means to let everyone know what they were planning to do when the time is right."

Scarlett offered a grim smile. "That sounds perfect."

Lin came up and grabbed their arms. "Pay attention, you two. Amber just said it's time to go, right now. Police on the way."

Wren called, "Vacate, immediate," and Scarlett ran with the rest toward the rally points where portals to safety awaited.

CHAPTER TWENTY-ONE

The rush to get everyone back to the warehouse was hectic and confusing, but it sorted itself out relatively quickly. After doing what she could to help, Scarlett headed for her locker and changed into a pair of sweatpants and a sweatshirt she had borrowed from Lin some time before for this possibility. She went to the sink and washed her face, pulled her hair into a messy ponytail, and headed back out to the main room.

Her gaze shifted toward the interrogation area, where she knew Crimson Robe's right-hand man was currently being stored, but she wasn't ready to deal with him. Besides that, Wren was still officially in charge of the goings-on, and she was away.

Scarlett located Amber sitting at a small table on the first floor rather than up in her infomancer area, typing on a small laptop. Scarlett sat beside her, and Runeclaw jumped up and rubbed his chin against the side of the screen. Amber absently scratched his ears with her gaze locked on whatever she saw on her computer. Scarlett asked, "What's up?"

"Watching the mansion from high above. The drone's still there. Also monitoring police radios and communications, at least the unencrypted ones. My systems are working on the encryption they're using. That's probably SWAT since they're on the scene as well."

"Any sign of trouble?"

The infomancer shook her head. "It's basically a bunch of officials milling around looking for something to do now that they missed the real action. The important people we left tied up have been sent away in their limos, doubtless to be deluged with requests to show up at the station for an interview they will decline forever through their lawyers."

Scarlett snorted at the comment but frowned. "I don't like how easy they got off. I'd vote for all of them to be in jail for a while."

Amber flashed an evil smile. "Don't worry. I'll be spending my free time compiling all the dirt I can on every one of them. When the time is right, they'll get theirs in a very nasty, very public way."

Lin sat across from Scarlett. "They better. It took all I had not to shoot them before we left. Scumbags."

Runeclaw replied, "It does seem like the world might be better off without some people in it."

Scarlett poked him. "You're not allowed to become an assassin. Just know that's off the table."

He gave her a condescending look. "Don't worry, no one will kill you. We'll keep you around for comedic purposes."

She poked him again, and he swatted at her hand with soft paws rather than claws. Wren walked up, looking tired., "Everyone still okay? No post-op jitters?"

Lin replied, "None here."

Scarlett confirmed, "None here, either. Regret for not beating on those jerks some before we left, but no jitters."

Lin asked, "What's going on, boss?"

Wren took the remaining seat at the square table. "The captives were all fine, but Snow is worried about what the Veil might make them do now that they're out in the world. They are wearing mind-control collars, after all. The doctors at the hospital have them all sedated for the moment, but that's not a long-term solution."

Lin muttered a curse. "Rescued, only to be kept unconscious. Not awesome."

"Not at all."

Scarlett asked, "What can we do to help?"

Wren shrugged. Frustration was evident in her tone. "I really don't know, especially given what you said someone told you about anti-magic emitters. That would've been my first thought without the warning. Snow's on it. Hopefully he'll come up with something."

The moment hung for several seconds of silence as they all contemplated the situation. Then Wren said, "Now, tell me about your half of the operation."

Scarlett replied, "Taking the limo was easy. Emma did really well. The disguises worked to get us inside, and I don't think anyone knew we were trouble until we dispelled them. The people were a weird mix. All of them had assistants or partners with them like it was an ordinary social occasion. Most of them seemed unspeakably arrogant, although a few appeared less so."

Lin added, "Probably those were the ones who left early without a servant."

"Probably. And good for them. How are they?"

Wren replied, "Safe and sound. The Spell Riders intercepted them. No harm."

"Good." Scarlett went back to her retelling. "When you guys made your move, Camus and Trane ran, along with the guy we've got in the back. When we chased them, Lin wasn't paying attention and got herself shot."

Lin slapped a hand on the table. "Lies, I tell you, lies. He saw me as the more dangerous opponent who needed to be taken out first. He was behind you, too, if you recall."

Scarlett laughed. "Yeah, I'm sure that's what it was. Definitely that."

Lin glared at her, and Scarlett stuck her tongue out at the other woman. "Anyway, I got downstairs and held my own against the two of them, but no more than that. Runeclaw broke the stalemate. We killed Trane, but Camus got away through some door in the wall."

Wren shook her head. "That stupid wall. Once the police were done down there, we smuggled a couple of people in to take a look. Quietly, since the authorities are still on the scene. We can't get through there, even with explosives. They detected a heavy, not completely magical shield somehow embedded in the wall, possibly a fundamental part of the structure. Either way, no getting through."

Scarlett replied, "Annoying."

"It really is."

Lin added, "He surely portaled away immediately, in any case. If there were any secrets in there, by now, they aren't there anymore."

Runeclaw interjected, "We've broken his plans into tiny bits, I would imagine. It will take some time to regroup if he can do so at all."

Scarlett reminded them, "There are almost certainly still collared people out there."

Wren nodded. "I know. Snow's working on that, too. In the meantime, shall we go have a chat with our captive?"

They agreed that would be a good idea. The three of them plus Runeclaw headed for interrogation while Amber detoured toward the stairs that led up to her workspace.

Wren opened the door, and Scarlett stepped inside. The man was shackled to the single metal chair in the bare lighting and looked resigned. His hair stuck up in all directions, but other than that, he managed to appear dignified even in these dire straits. Wren asked, "Your name?"

"Ellis."

"Is that first or last?"

"Only."

Lin laughed. "Like Madonna? Prince?"

The side of his mouth twitched up in a smile. "Yes, exactly. My stardom should be evident."

Scarlett laughed at the droll humor, impressed that he could pull it off in this situation. "Well, Ellis, tell us. Were there more collared people than we saw at the gathering?"

"There were. Probably two dozen, more or less. Each of the members of the Veil has one, plus other powerful people. You interrupted the last gathering. There were others."

Wren asked, "What plans does the Veil have for them?"

Ellis shrugged. "Above my pay grade."

Lin snorted. "Please. You were Camus' right-hand man. You know more than that."

"He had plans. That's all I can say. I wasn't privy to them."

Wren asked, "Where's the organization's money held?"

He laughed. "All over the place, and you're not going to find it. The Veil hires smart and pays well."

Scarlett countered, "Yet you lost. Speaking of losers, where's Camus run away to?"

"Our defensive plan was to get him down to his room. After that, he was on his own. He's a wizard. Can portal. All we needed to do was get him to a temporary safe place."

"How many others are there in the organization? Who's the leader now?"

Ellis inclined his head. "Camus *is* the group, thanks to you. The ones he didn't kill because they were untrustworthy, you eliminated. The Luminous Veil is done, for all intents and purposes."

They all exchanged glances. Lin asked, "You really expect us to believe you're not just covering for your boss?"

He shrugged. "Doesn't matter to me what you believe. I can only tell you what I know, and that's what I know. He's the last wizard standing."

They spent twenty minutes more re-asking the same questions and some others that occurred to them but gained no more information. Eventually, they wandered back out into the main room of the warehouse. Wren left to get some sleep, and Scarlett asked, "What next?"

Lin replied, "Not sure. Guess we'll see. I think the decisions come from Wren."

"Should've grabbed a couple more people to interrogate."

Lin nodded. "Bringing Trane back would've been good. Did Fang influence your strike?"

Scarlett shook her head. "No. After seeing those people in the collars being offered up like that, we agreed on the location of that particular strike. Camus would've met the same fate if we caught him."

"Hopefully you'll get another chance."

"We better." Scarlett sighed. "Come on, Runeclaw. We should rest up while we can. I'm guessing whatever Snow comes up with will involve us."

Lin replied, "Good plan. Think I'll do that too."

Shortly after, Scarlett was showered and under the covers with Runeclaw lying beside her on the bedspread. He observed, "Our mission was a win, even though it doesn't really feel like one."

"I know. I just wish we could've gotten Camus. I'm worried about what he'll do with those collars."

"No matter how much you'd like to, you can't control that, so let it go."

Scarlett closed her eyes and nestled into her pillows. "Wise words, Guardian."

Runeclaw put his head down on his paws. "As always."

CHAPTER TWENTY-TWO

The next morning, Scarlett sat in Wheels with a cup of coffee in her hand and Runeclaw on her lap. The workers were doing their construction thing all around the interior, but most importantly, the urn had been replaced, and the coffee was plentiful. She was relaxing with her feet up on a second chair and her eyes closed when someone with a baritone voice commented, "I think she's dead."

Scarlett grinned. "I am. But if you think you're taking Dusk Runner away, you're wrong. She'll be buried with me."

Maddox and Snow laughed as Scarlett opened her eyes and dropped her feet. Snow replied, "That is the correct answer."

Wren walked over. "Good, you're finally here."

It took Scarlett a second to realize she was talking to the men, not to her.

Maddox answered, "We just came from the hospital. Everything's fine. But Snow here has an idea." The way he said the last word made Scarlett think it would be turbulent waters ahead.

Snow nodded. "I do, but I need coffee first." Everyone took seats as he got himself and Maddox a mug, then sat. "All right. I think I've got a way to use the collar we already have to get the other collars off. But it's going to be dangerous, it's going to be difficult, and at a bare minimum, it's going to require all our combined power to pull it off."

Wren stated, "We're in."

"All the Witches. All the Riders. No one exempt."

"Like I said, we're in."

Scarlett asked, "Why so much?"

Snow replied, "We need to do all the collars at once to prevent the Veil from reacting to us breaking some but not others. I have no idea what they might do, if they can do anything, or if they'll even notice, but we can't afford to risk it."

Wren replied, "That seems logical."

Lin walked up and grabbed a seat. "What seems logical?"

Snow got her up to speed, then continued. "The Spell Riders will prepare the ritual area. I'd like the Witches to move the patients from the hospital. You won't be able to portal directly there, so you'll need to get stretchers to carry them up the path. You won't be able to roll them, but magic should work."

Wren nodded. "That's not a problem, but it won't take all of us. What do you want the rest to do?"

He closed his eyes, and Scarlett thought he looked tired. It was possible he'd been up all night trying to figure this out. Another look at him made her change that from possible to probable. "Whoever is best at ritual magic should get to the site and help prepare the ground by exchanging energy with it to bring the available power closer to the surface."

Wren nodded. "Makes sense. We can do that."

"Finally, drones nearby to watch for trouble."

Lin grinned. "Amber will know how to provide security and will enjoy doing it. Have no worries on that count."

Snow nodded. "All right. Let's get moving, then. Everything needs to be in place before dusk."

Scarlett and Lin got to work right away. One of the Witches portaled them to the hospital, and they took charge of the unconscious patients. Scarlett handled the IV stand while Lin floated the patient. They carried their burden through a portal to the clearing where the Spell Riders and the Witches on Wheels had gotten together before, then found the path, watched over by one of the Spell Riders.

He waved them forward. "The last one went up about a minute ago, so you shouldn't have any problems."

They floated their burden up to the clearing used for ritual magic. When they arrived, Snow pointed. "Same distance as the others, inner ring."

The patients who had already arrived had been positioned almost like spokes on a wheel around the central area at the distance of the first stone ring. Scarlett could picture the finished arrangement, which would have the unconscious people arranged symmetrically all the way around.

One of the Spell Riders made a force cushion in the

appropriate spot, and they lowered their burden onto it. Scarlett set the IV stand next to it, and the man advised, "We'll leave this for now, but it'll have to go before we start. That much metal right next to the bodies will be a problem for the magic."

Scarlett nodded. "Whatever you say." She and Lin headed back for the next body.

It took them and the other Witches working to transfer the patients four trips to get them all there. By then, it was early afternoon.

Snow buzzed around, ensuring everything was as it should be. Scarlett had never seen him so frenetic. He was normally calm and collected. Now, he seemed like he was in a race, and only by constantly expending as much energy as possible could he win. She and Lin did what they could to help him.

The clearing filled up as the day passed and people finished their tasks. Scarlett asked if she should join in with the outer ring, where the ritual magic experts exchanged energy with the land. Snow said no, that task was best suited to people with the appropriate training. She continued to make herself useful as best she could until finally, Snow left the area for a while, then came back carrying the box with the collar inside.

He took it to the small, raised pedestal in the center of the ritual arrangement and called, "Everyone into position." Several Spell Riders helped out, getting everyone into their proper spots. Then Snow held up a large goblet engraved with various symbols. It was silver, or perhaps steel, and shone with a high polish.

Snow pulled out a small knife, nicked his thumb, and

squeezed blood into the goblet. Maddox did the same a moment later, then made his way through the crowd, piercing each person and adding their blood to the mix. When everyone had donated, he brought the cup back to Snow.

The Spell Riders' artificer held it in one hand and waved his wand above it in the other, chanting words in a harsh tongue Scarlett didn't recognize. The tempo and volume of his chant increased until he shouted a final command. A ripple of power washed out from the center, and he smiled. "It's ready."

Maddox called, "Every stone needs a dab of blood. Every collar needs one, as well. We'll pass the chalice around." As it circled, Lin muttered, "Lot more rocks here now than there were before." They knew that was true since they'd assisted in placing them earlier in the day.

Scarlett asked, "I can't remember. Did the ones we used before have runes like the ones we laid down today?"

Lin shook her head. "No. I've never seen the ones with runes. Which means this really is much bigger magic than the other stuff we've done, and probably that Snow was up all night making carved rocks."

Scarlett winced. "That doesn't sound like fun."

"It does not."

When they finished, Snow gave instructions in a voice that brooked no argument. He told everyone to shield, then detailed individual people to be responsible for one of the collared captives. They were to shield them, then shield their collars separately, all the way around the metal band.

He chose Scarlett to do so for one of them, and she

created the shields and locked them in place in a corner of her mind. She added one for Runeclaw, as well.

Snow ordered, "Now, we must connect our energies, just like we did before. Connect with the person next to you on the left. In that way, we'll circle and connect everyone together in a big spiral out from the center. The collared people won't be part of it unless I can somehow access their minds, but that's doubtful."

Scarlett relaxed and listened to the flow of his words as he chanted again. As before, whatever magic he summoned guided her to extend her power to the next person and to welcome the connection from Lin, who was on her right. She used her familiarity with Runeclaw's pendant to add him into the mix. The feeling of building power was palpable inside her body and outside it, in the air and the earth. She saw from others' faces that they felt it too.

Once the connections were fully established, Snow instructed, "Focus on my words." He continued to chant, making sounds Scarlett couldn't process. She soon breathed differently and realized she was doing so in time with everyone else. They were like one large organism operating in unison.

Snow gave them more instructions. "Okay. When I begin this, I will link to the collars. Everyone focus on your connection to one another and send the power toward me, toward those collars. I will draw energy from you as I need it. Do not let me take too much. Fall out of the circle before you take any damage because we're working at a level where that damage could be potentially fatal."

His chant quickened, and Scarlett knew that given the

life-or-death stakes for the collared captives, neither she nor anyone else would follow that advice unless they were on death's doorstep.

CHAPTER TWENTY-THREE

Scarlett felt the feather touch of Snow's magic on her power. Like the previous time she'd taken part in his ritual magic, her mind followed the power toward him, passing around the spiral until suddenly she saw what he did. He held the collar she had found, now fully polished and pristine. Whatever damage had been done the previous time, if any, had been repaired.

He turned it around in his hands and ran them over the object as if checking its surface for impurities. Her fingers tingled with the sensation as if they were the ones touching it.

Scarlett was cognizant of being in three places or being three people at once. Herself, in the crowd. Snow, in the center. And the giant entity their blending of power had created. She sensed the familiar touch of Lin's magic and Runeclaw's. Those combined with all the others and fit together perfectly in the amalgam Snow had created.

The artificer continued to chant. Although her mouth wasn't moving, it was as if her voice was added to the mix like everyone else's, all emanating from Snow's throat. He barked a word, then snarled another, and their perception changed. It was as if they flew into the collar, shrinking along the way to slip between the molecules.

It would have been frightening if it hadn't been familiar. It had scared and thrilled her the last time they did this. The mad strands of magical metal were woven through the collar they stood within, with the non-magical stuff interposed so the magical metals didn't touch. They looked like tree limbs on Halloween or veins of glowing light against a night sky.

As he had last time, Snow thoroughly examined the interior elements, tracing the path of one magical metal, then the other, and finally the remaining metals. His attention turned to the spells that held the arrangement together, the ones he had previously teased apart to understand the thing.

Now, his actions were different. He pressed, pulled, and used his magic to separate and bring together the metals. After each effort, he paused to gauge the reaction from the collar. He did the same with each spell in turn, pushing on their boundaries.

As he engaged with each element, Scarlett understood it like he did, a depth of knowledge and insight that fascinated her. She wondered if that was his magic, his artificer training, or his intelligence. *Probably some of each, like with most things.* Then her mind was back on task.

Snow sent a thought to all of them that hit her ears like words. *The goal is to break the links inside the collar, to make the metals no longer resonate the way they do. I think if I do that prop-*

erly, the collars will crack. If I don't do it properly, there's no telling what might happen. My guess is they could shatter violently, which would be bad for the people who aren't currently shielded.

Another thought, Maddox's, drawled, *So be careful.*

Snow chuckled. *Focus now.*

The inner metal bulged and shifted in Scarlett's vision as Snow manipulated it. It slid farther between the two magical metals, pushing on them. Since they didn't have room to move, the action created dents in each. He solidified the non-magical metal, holding it in place to fill those dents. Scarlett felt a vibration hum through her as the collar's resonance changed. Her stomach felt suddenly nauseous as the timbre of the spells inside the collar also changed. Every sense told her that something was wrong.

Snow snarled, "Dammit, too much." He pulled the inert metal mostly away, leaving only the slightest indentation remaining in the magical metals, and the vibration settled to a small buzz. It differed from what it had originally been, but not markedly so. The spells accepted this new normal and returned to their former quiescent state.

Snow repeated the process elsewhere in the collar, and also tried moving the magical metal. That effort created a disproportionate reaction. After trying it once with each kind, he focused on the inert metal instead, warping it and changing its path in places. Again, after each alteration, he paused to judge the effect of doing so. Finally, he thought, *Okay. I see what I need to do now. This will be difficult. Brace yourselves.*

Everyone drew in a breath together. Then Snow pulled power from the group in earnest. Energy flowed into her, through her, and past her. She was suffused with it and at the same time couldn't hold onto it.

Stars filled her vision, slowly at first but faster as the energy seeped out of her body. Her head felt woozy, but she forced herself to focus through the sensation. Through the link with Runeclaw, she felt her partner stagger and immediately broke the connection and severed him from the group. He'd doubtless argue with her about the choice later, but at least he'd be alive to do so. Hopefully she would still be alive to listen.

The change in their shared being when several other people dropped out of it in the next minutes made Scarlett's pulse quicken and her thoughts turn frantic. They couldn't let the spell fail, but it seemed like there wasn't enough power available to feed it. She reached deep into the well of power she held and sent her magic questing beyond it, out into the world. Her grandmother's pendant, which she always wore against her skin, began to burn and the smell of her grandmother's perfume filled her nostrils.

Lin fell out of the arrangement, along with several more people, and the moment teetered on the edge of disaster. Then, through the pendant, Scarlett felt a link snap into place. Power flowed from the earth below her, up through her, and toward Snow.

She wasn't controlling it. She was only a node, a piece of the road the power traveled to reach the artificer. A cog in an arcane machine. There was so much of it available, waiting to be drawn. This must be what the others had been building and channeling toward Snow throughout the ritual. With her late grandmother's help, she found a way to be part of that connection.

A moment later, a blinding ripple that spread out from the center of the ritual clearing struck Scarlett's eyes. It knocked her and everyone else backward to the ground. She lay there feeling entirely broken and empty for several moments, then gasped as her power returned, flowing into her and restoring her. She realized then that she'd heard a loud snap as the wave had come out.

She got to her feet and looked at the former captives. Their collars hung open. The sound had been them breaking. They were still unconscious, still sedated, but they were free.

Scarlett turned to help Lin to her feet, then checked on Runeclaw and carried him with her as she headed toward the center. Snow sat cross-legged on the pedestal. The collar was back in its protective box. He looked drawn out and exhausted, and she was pretty sure the hair that hung into his face was whiter than it had been when they'd started the ritual. She asked, "What just happened?"

He smiled. "We managed to push the magical metals far enough apart all the way around that the collar's internal structure failed. Because we were careful about how we did it and ensured the most important binding spells weren't affected, it snapped between two particularly strong spells I set up to resonate against one another rather than shattering."

Scarlett shook her head. "You're a madman. Brilliant, clearly. But a madman."

Snow chuckled. "You're not the first person to say so. I highly doubt you will be the last."

Maddox said in a voice that was as hoarse as if he'd

been shouting for an hour, "She won't. Because I'm saying it too."

Several other voices nearby joined in, and Snow waved. "Shut up. All of you."

Scarlett asked, "And the collars that weren't here in the circle?"

Snow ran his fingers through his hair and shook his head. "I can't be sure, but it shouldn't hurt them. Hopefully, it had enough power to reach all the collars and snap them open. What happens from there I can't say. But I'm hopeful, and I am certain we did all we could do."

He raised an eyebrow at her. "And you did more. I felt it. What happened there?"

Scarlett shook her head. "I don't know. Somehow, the pendant my grandmother bequeathed to me made a connection with the power under the earth and used me as a channel."

"Well, if I were you, I'd keep that pendant close at hand forever."

"Right? I will definitely do that."

Wren walked up. "What should we do with these folks?" She gestured at the unconscious people in the broken collars.

Snow replied, "Take off those collars and collect them. We need to put them in a magically neutral box or protected space since we don't know whether the Veil can still use them. I don't think they can since what I did should've also broken the magic, but let's not take any risks. Then, let's get those folks back to the hospital. No more sedation, though." He beamed as he said the last sentence.

Wren grinned and clapped him on the shoulder. "Perfect. Well done, Snow."

Scarlett laughed. "Why is everyone being so nice to him? His ego's going to be enormous."

Runeclaw muttered from where he nestled against her chest, "And Scarlett can't handle the competition with her humongous one."

"If you weren't so broken down, cat, I would slap you."

He mumbled, "Bring it," then immediately fell asleep.

Scarlett patted his head. "Goofball."

Lin came up. "Go take care of your cat. I'll handle getting this bunch where they belong. Be sure to sleep in because tomorrow, we're gonna have a celebration like Wheels hasn't seen in a long time."

Scarlett nodded, but before she headed out of the ritual circle, she stepped close to Snow. "Truly well done. Thank you."

He nodded and with the same seriousness, replied, "My pleasure."

CHAPTER TWENTY-FOUR

Scarlett slept late the next morning, as instructed, then spent the rest of the day helping with the reconstruction of Wheels. At least, she thought she was helping. Runeclaw suggested the correct word was "hindering."

By the time the work stopped at five, the inner walls were done, the floor was finished, and the tables and benches were coming along well. Most importantly, the bar and all its connections were back in place, which meant the locals had returned.

Scarlett helped Lin with the bartending, served some tables, and generally had a good time interacting with customers and club members in the lighthearted, positive atmosphere. The stress, anger, and rage had been burned away by their success last night. Or maybe by the energy that had flowed through her during the ritual.

She still didn't understand what had happened, but after worrying about it for a while, she'd put it away. She didn't need to know. She would continue to wear the locket. Maybe nothing like that would ever occur again, but it had happened when it was needed, and that was what mattered.

In the early evening, Amber arrived with an update on the hospital patients. All were fully conscious again and were generally healthy. The collars didn't appear to have caused any lasting damage. Some had been captives for longer and had stories to tell, although their memories were murky, doubtless from the magic.

The Spell Riders were handling the interface with the FBI, who handled kidnappings, and would escort the former captives in for interviews. It wouldn't happen until they were mentally ready and had gotten enough rest to be up to the challenge, and not without the lawyers the Spell Riders provided. The Riders and Witches had rescued these folks, which instilled the burden of caring for them until they were back to normal.

Scarlett idly wondered as she cleaned up a table whether normal was possible for them again. Or for her. She certainly wasn't the person she'd been when she came to Earth from Oriceran. It had been quite a journey, but she'd come out the other end mostly unscathed, and who could complain about that?

Runeclaw hopped onto the table, slid on the wetness, and knocked a saltshaker off it. She caught it and scowled. "Maybe be careful, klutz?"

"Maybe learn to clean?" His counter was saucy. Whatever had happened to him the night before hadn't lasted. He was very much back to his normal, deeply annoying self.

A ruckus at the door caught her attention, and Scarlett turned to see several Witches working together to maneuver a large object through the opening. Once it was inside, they used their wands to cut the box apart. It fell away to reveal a pair of electronic dartboards that used darts without points. Which, to be fair, was probably safest, given this crowd.

They floated them up to the back wall, plugged them in, and marked off the line for throwing.

Scarlett leaned on the bar. "Nice upgrade."

Lin chuckled. "It was time. We've got a couple of those retro arcade units on the way too, ones with all the old games. Pac-Man, Asteroids, Space Invaders, everything."

"What's next, a trivia night? Karaoke?"

Lin grinned. "I don't know. Maybe. Guess we'll see how everyone takes to this. Now, back to work, slacker." Scarlett laughed and did as she was told.

Eventually, she shifted from worker to reveler. The place was full to the brim with Spell Riders and Witches on Wheels, plus several locals who had decided not to leave or heard about the party and came to be a part of it. Her turn at the dartboard arrived and she pulled Snow over with her. They threw several darts, and she frowned at how much better his throws were than hers. "You know, I've heard about the lawn darts."

He scowled. "From Maddox, I'm sure. Lies, spread by those who are big losers at lawn darts." He yelled the last words loud enough for them to carry to where Maddox stood talking to Wren ten feet away.

The leader of the Spell Riders waved a negligent hand in Snow's direction.

After several more throws, the artificer had defeated her soundly. "You cheat, sir."

He laughed. "I will admit, I have a competitive streak. But I definitely do not cheat. I mean, it's not like I needed to."

Scarlett's mouth made a perfect O. "Wicked burn. Uncool."

He laughed.

Runeclaw interjected, "It's okay, Scarlett. This is just one more thing to put on the long list of stuff you're bad at."

She pointed at him. "You, cat, are a jerk. Shut your little cat mouth."

"How about I bite you with my little cat teeth instead?"

She looked at him, then at Snow. "Maybe you two should be partners. You're perfect for each other." She stalked away from them and spent some time talking to Lin.

Their conversation was interrupted when Wren stepped onto the bar and shouted for quiet. "First piece of good news. Wheels is now open for business again."

Everyone cheered.

"We've made some improvements, and we'll make some more, but it's good to have the place back." Several people loudly agreed. "Next, our friends in the hospital will all be okay. No ill effects. The doctors are sure of it."

More cheering circled the room.

Lin commented, "Thank goodness for that."

Scarlett nodded. "Definitely."

Then Wren yelled, "Finally, we owe this success to Snow. Everyone give him a hand." He lifted two fists in a dramatic victory pose, and the place erupted in applause and laughter.

Hours later, as the evening was winding down, Scarlett sat at a table with Amber, Lin, and Runeclaw. One of the improvements Wren had mentioned was mounting a large television in the back corner of the place, and it caught their attention as a news report came across the screen with an image of a collar over the newscaster's shoulder. Amber hit some buttons to increase the volume.

The anchor said, "Tonight we have a follow-up on the missing students from our area and elsewhere, who have suddenly returned home with stories of being kidnapped."

The woman went on to explain the details they had, which weren't many. The students said they'd been captured and collars had been put around their necks. Their memory of what happened next was fuzzy, although they all recalled being used as labor of one kind or another.

Then one day, all the collars snapped open simultaneously for no apparent reason. The captives had run away, fear of what the collars had done to them pushing them to escape. Neighbors, police, and Good Samaritans had picked them up.

Lin observed, "All right. More good news. Perfect way to end the day." They'd heard bits about it earlier in the day, but this report had the most information. Lin called, "Time for our press release?"

From where she stood leaning on the bar beside Maddox, Wren shouted, "Amber, make it so."

The infomancer hit some buttons on her computer, and a couple of minutes later, the anchor interrupted the story they were telling.

"This just in. We've received information from an

anonymous source about a number of prominent politicians and business leaders who were apparently involved in the disappearances of those who were taken and collared. We can't say more before vetting the information, but our team is hard at work doing that now, and we promise to get you up to date as soon as we can. Stay with us."

Scarlett asked, "What did you send?"

The infomancer grinned. "Video. Audio. Emails. Whatever I and the people I hired could find on those jerks. It might not put them in jail, but it should mess up their lives really well."

The party continued into the early morning hours. Finally, when everyone's eyes were drooping, Lin asked her, "So now what?"

Scarlett replied, "Now that we've defeated the Veil? Hard to top that. I think it's time to hit the road again."

Runeclaw, who had been napping on the table throughout, opened one eye. "What stupid place are you planning to take me to this time?"

Scarlett laughed and gave him an affectionate pat. "I thought we might see some national treasures along the way. Stick around the Grand Canyon and hike for a while. That kind of thing."

His gaze turned suspicious. "You're lying."

She put a hand on her chest and tried to look innocent. "I'm not. How could you?"

"Ghosts of the Grand Canyon. I can see it now."

The entire table laughed, and she replied, "No." She turned her attention to Lin and Amber. "You could come along. Take a little vacation. Do some riding. Hang out."

Lin gave a decisive nod. "I'm in. A vacation sounds great."

Amber shook her head. "I'll live vicariously through you. Just be sure to wear your glasses so I can see and hear what you do."

Scarlett replied, "You sure? It'll be fun, I promise."

Amber nodded. "I'm sure, but thanks."

As Scarlett got up to leave, Lin whispered, "I'll work on her. She'll come."

With only good thoughts in her mind, Scarlett portaled back to the hotel, where she and Runeclaw snuggled into bed and fell asleep with pleasant thoughts of the days to come.

CHAPTER TWENTY-FIVE

While her dreams were uniformly pleasant, Scarlett's awakening was anything but. Her phone shrilled with the signal that something was wrong. She grabbed it and coughed out, "What?"

Amber tersely advised, "There's trouble. Get to Mystic Realms. The street outside it, I mean, not the building itself."

Scarlett wondered why the infomancer felt the need to add that last part as she pulled on her boots and grabbed her jacket. She opened a portal and stepped through to a scene of chaos. The building that held the comic book store was fully aflame and had been for some time.

Scarlett sent her magic into the building to search for people, for anything, but found nothing but heat and flame. Fire trucks poured water on the blaze, but it didn't dissipate. She drew her wand, summoned frost magic, and dropped it on the nearest part of the conflagration, but it proved strangely resistant to dousing. She continued, focusing her full power on it, and finally, after twenty minutes or so, their combined efforts put out the fire.

Scarlett coated herself with force shields and raced into the structure despite the warnings from the firefighters. The shop's main room held no bodies, only tons of burned comics, books, and games. She bashed through the door into the back area, fearing she'd find the bodies of her friends. It too was empty, although as fully destroyed as the outer area.

She wandered back outside in a daze, her brain not fully processing what was going on around her, and called Amber. "No one was in there."

The infomancer let out a loud sigh. "Thank goodness. Okay, get over here when you can." The call dropped.

Scarlett looked around for Runeclaw, then realized she must've closed the portal before he could follow her through. She returned to her hotel, dumped her smoky clothes in a corner, and took a cold shower to wake herself up. She shivered as she dressed again, then portaled to the warehouse. Runeclaw raced ahead as she ran up the stairs to Amber's workspace.

The infomancer was leaning forward in her chair to stare at videos playing back on her monitors from several different sources. She pointed at them. "As near as I can tell, these videos have the regulars going in through the back late last night. They'd been staying there overnight lately, based on the recordings, and leaving in the mornings. I don't know why. But I don't have any evidence of them leaving before the fire."

"Well, they definitely weren't in there. No information from the local hospitals?"

"I'll keep checking, but nothing so far. I mean, that's good news, right?"

Scarlett scowled. The anger inside her wanted to burst forth in a scream. "So, this was what, a vendetta by Crimson Robe? Payback?"

Runeclaw replied, "Or a message."

Scarlett fell into a chair and took several deep breaths to calm herself. When she had a handle on her temper, she requested, "Show me again."

They went through the videos frame by frame, but there was nothing to indicate that what they saw was an illusion. It looked like her friends had gone into the back room the night before and not come out. Yet they hadn't been there during the fire.

Scarlett rubbed her eyes. "So, anything could've happened to them. Including portaling away, I guess."

Amber asked, "They haven't replied?"

Scarlett shook her head. "No. I used the danger code, so they should have. Have you located their phones?"

"No." Then she frowned. "Wait. I got a ping from one now. It must've started in the last few minutes while we've been focused on the videos."

Scarlett shot to her feet. "Where?"

Amber rotated to face her with a look of concern. "The Driskill Hotel."

The news hit her like a lightning bolt. It confirmed this was an attack aimed at her. She was the only connection between her friends and the Driskill.

Scarlett ran into the back of the warehouse and pulled off her jacket. She slipped on the harness with the knives that were hidden by her hair and her wrist sheaths with the other ones. Next, she positioned her bandolier over Fang's harness and shoved her pistol into its waistband holster. Then she opened a portal to the street outside the Driskill Hotel.

She stomped inside and angled toward the staircase.

Amber stated, "Fifth floor."

Scarlett pulled the revolver and carried it openly as soon as she was out of sight. She encountered no one as she took the five flights three stairs at a time and stopped a short distance from the indicated room.

Runeclaw asked, "Subtlety?"

Scarlett snarled, "Hardly," and blasted the door open. She dashed inside with the gun raised but found only the phone Amber was tracking and a box wrapped like a present, just big enough to hold in two hands.

Amber was looking through the camera in her glasses. She warned, "Be careful."

"I know. I'm angry, but I'm not stupid." The fact that Runeclaw didn't take the opportunity to disagree with her underscored the seriousness of the situation.

She created a force shield around the phone and floated it away from the box. Another force shield went between her and the box, and yet another around the box. She left a tiny hole to work through and unwrapped it with twitches of force magic.

The box held a metallic cube with a button on the top. She moved the box out of the way in its force shield and set the cube on the bed. Then she used force magic to press the button.

A flickering appeared and quickly resolved to a holographic image of a man she recognized. She snarled, "Camus."

He nodded. His eyes showed anger, but his demeanor was neutral. "Scarlett Prynne. A pleasure to meet you wearing your face this time."

She offered him a thin smile. "The pleasure's all yours, believe me. Where are my friends?"

He gestured, and the image panned to the left. Anders, Aldrin, Sia, and Tia were all nearby, standing rigid against the wall, clearly held there by magic. Only their eyes moved, and she got nothing useful from them. Scarlett said, "They're not involved."

Camus laughed condescendingly. "Well, they wouldn't be if not for you, but I'm afraid they are. I mean, you broke into my house, attacked me, and ruined a very pleasant and potentially profitable evening. Shouldn't I have some recompense for all that?"

"Tell me what you want. I'll give it to you when you let them go."

He laughed. "Yes, I'll certainly trust you." He paused as if reconsidering. "Oh, wait, no I won't. So, here's what we're going to do. I offer you a challenge. A fight to the death, you and I. Well, you can bring your cat. He's caused me no end of trouble as well." He waved toward his captives. "No other riffraff will be involved. Just you two and me. And when you're dead, I promise not to go after them."

Scarlett growled, "What guarantee do I have that you'll keep your promise?"

"Why, none. But you have no opportunity to save them without accepting it, which leaves you in something of a bind, doesn't it?"

She gritted her teeth. "Name the time and place."

Camus nodded. "Tonight. Midnight. Take this cube with you. It will open a portal at the appointed time."

"How do I know it's not a bomb or something?"

He waved again. "Shield it, put it out in a field, do whatever you need to do with it except put it near an anti-magic emitter. It will work as it's intended to. I have no desire to blow you up. I'd much rather kill you personally."

"I'm supposed to just come through that portal?"

"Yes. Like I said, I want to see your blood run so there won't be any tricks with the portal. And don't even think to play games with me."

Scarlett didn't like the setup, but he held all the cards. For now. "And the captives?"

"Will be with me. You may bring one friend to take them home."

"So, no witnesses to this fight, huh? Truly just us and you?"

"You, me, and the cat. A fight to the death. For all the marbles, as they say."

Scarlett snarled, "You're on."

He inclined his head. "Until then." The camera panned to show her friends again, then the image vanished.

Scarlett wrapped more shields around the cube. She didn't trust his word that it wasn't a bomb.

Runeclaw warned, "This is a bad idea. You know it won't be a fair fight."

Scarlett scrubbed her face with her hands. "I know it's a bad idea and he'll cheat, somehow. But I don't see any other way to save them. Do you?" She hoped for a different answer than she received.

"No. So, we'll just have to meet him and kill him."

"Yes. That's exactly what we need to do."

Amber interjected, "At least you've got the day to prepare. I'd suggest you use every minute of it figuring out a way to turn the tables on that bastard."

Scarlett choked out a dark laugh. "Oh, I plan to. I'll bring this junk back to the warehouse. Do you have a place we can store this thing safely?"

"No, so we'll need to put it outside. But we can have people watch it every second."

"Good enough. On my way."

CHAPTER TWENTY-SIX

Camus strolled through the upstairs hallway of the darkened house. This refuge was his alone, unconnected to the Veil. He'd bought it early in his life and erased the records of his ownership.

Located in the suburbs of Salt Lake City, it was indistinguishable from the houses around it. Computer systems and short-term employees had handled making it look occasionally inhabited. This was the first time he'd spent significant time in the place, and it was dismal compared to his mansion.

He opened the door to the master bedroom and glanced at the figures on the bed. His magic still held all the witch's friends rigid. The spell was segmented to a corner of his mind but always functioning. He couldn't sleep while keeping it active, but that wasn't a problem since meditation didn't break the link and was sufficient.

He smiled thinly at them. "I'm sure your friend will come through for you. She's certainly the type. If she does, I'll keep my word and let you go."

They didn't respond. They couldn't while locked in his spell. He closed the door and headed down two flights of stairs to the basement. He cast a similar ritual to the one he used in his mansion to open a hole in the wall, then stepped through.

This sanctuary was about half the size of the other, but it now held his wardrobe, bookshelves, and armor suit. He'd portaled them over immediately upon escaping the witch and her cat and was glad to have done so.

It had taken the authorities a few hours to get an anti-magic emitter positioned so he could no longer portal into the room, which gave him plenty of time to retrieve his essential items. His ritual circle here was only one ring, but it would still suffice. He knelt in the circle, activated the wards, and let his mind wander as it would.

Some time later, his mental clock informed him it was time to prepare. He rose and removed his robes. Underneath was a simple black turtleneck and black slacks. Over that, he donned his armor. First the scaled boots, then the trousers, and finally the breastplate and tunic.

He stretched and moved, reveling in how the metal shifted like silk on his body, although it was slightly heavy since he hadn't yet buffed his strength. The witch would have no idea of his level of protection, just like she had no idea about the other surprises that awaited her.

A wicked smile tugged at the corners of his mouth. He looked forward to the showdown and had been since the witch injected herself into his affairs. That reminder caused a flash of fury to blaze through his mind at the thought of everything she'd destroyed. He pushed it away with difficulty and focused on the present.

The past didn't matter, and the future still held promise. He could start over with the collars or think of some other plan to gain power. His story had much yet to be written. The witch's, on the other hand, would end in hours, accompanied by as much blood and pain as he could wring from her.

He drew his serpentine dagger from the wardrobe, examined it to ensure the poison in the tip was fresh, and slid it into the sheath at his belt. He slipped a healing potion and energy potion into their custom clips and added several other vials. Some might come in handy during the fight. Others would be a pleasure to use once the witch was immobilized, to deliver the maximum amount of pain possible before she died.

He donned his crimson robes and carefully arranged the folds to hide the armor. Then, almost religiously, he settled the helmet onto his head. This finishing touch made him feel every bit the warrior he was.

After reveling in the sensation, he removed it and attached it to a strap at the back of his belt. Finally, he reached into his wardrobe and withdrew his battle staff. His fingers explored the wood's knots and ridges in a ritual that always reacquainted him with it.

The staff had been carved from a single piece of wood, and the character of that thick branch remained. He had spent years pushing power into it and bonding it to him. It would serve him well tonight as it had so many times before. Finally, he slid his wand into the appropriate spot where it would connect with his battle staff and give him full access to all of his power.

Tonight would be the culmination of many things. Not

what he'd hoped for, had planned for. But finally, someone would see him in his true power and glory. The fact that she would die shortly thereafter was immaterial. He opened a portal to the bedroom upstairs, floated his captives through it, and carried them through another portal out onto the plateau.

Scarlett checked her watch. She had a half-hour to go before the pivotal moment. She'd delayed as long as she could and filled her time with things that didn't matter before coming to her locker. Lin stopped by and put a hand on her shoulder. "Do you need anything?"

Scarlett shook her head. "No. Just have to get dressed. Are you ready for tonight?"

The drow nodded. "I'll get your friends to safety, don't worry." Her footsteps receded, giving Scarlett the privacy she craved.

Scarlett wasn't worried about Camus' captives. Lin would handle it, and if her enemy decided to do something clever, they'd have to adapt as best they could. She looked at Runeclaw. "Guess it's time."

The cat nodded, uncommonly serious. "Guess it is."

Scarlett had already put on her base layer of black shirt and trousers and laced up her boots. Now she checked again to ensure her backup wand was in one boot. Lin had set a knife next to her on the bench sometime before, and Scarlett shoved it into the hidden scabbard in her other boot. She stood, stomped her feet to ensure neither object moved, then reached into her locker and drew out the bulletproof vest.

Lin's constant haranguing about it had finally worked. She didn't imagine she'd get shot at, but she believed every bit of defense she could get would be useful tonight and conceded that battle to her friend by strapping it on. It held two speed loaders for her revolver, but she doubted she'd have time for such luxuries as reloading.

Next, she slipped on her belt and cinched it tight. Her fingers found the grenades and potions on both sides and the enhanced technology and communication pack. She wouldn't have a connection with Amber tonight, but the pack would feed her display glasses reasonably well. She'd doubled up on her potions, one healing and one energy on each side of her belt. Lin would bring her own and wear her vest, Scarlett was sure.

Scarlett reached into the top of her locker, opened the box that held her pistol, and pulled it out. A press and flick opened the cylinder, and she verified it was loaded with anti-magic rounds. She closed it and slid it into the holster at the small of her back. She moved again, twisting and turning, and took several steps in each direction. Everything so far seemed balanced and adequately secured.

The clock in her head ticked off the seconds toward the moment of truth, which was simultaneously too soon and eternally far away.

She pulled the harness that held her long knives out of the locker and withdrew each blade to examine them. They'd been honed only a week before and not used since then, so they were ready. She shrugged into the harness, cinched the straps, and threw her hair back over it all to hide them, even though if Camus had researched her, he'd probably know she regularly carried them.

The wrist sheaths with their throwing knives went on next. She'd tested casting through them, and while the power loss was notable, she wouldn't refrain from using them because of it. Completing her blade deployment, she secured Fang's harness to the belt and ensured the dagger was secure.

Once again, she considered changing the poison in the dagger's tip from tranquilizer to something that would be fatal with a scratch. As she had several times already, she decided against it. One was as good as the other since it was long-lasting enough to keep anyone she hit down throughout the fight.

Finally, she added her last weapon, the bandolier with five tranquilizer darts that went over it all. She pulled on her leather jacket, left it unzipped, and checked to ensure her wand was up her sleeve where it was supposed to be. Naturally, it was. She turned to Runeclaw. "I'm ready."

He lifted his chin from where he sat on the bench. "Me too."

Scarlett laughed. "You're always ready. I have to put on all this stuff, and you're going as you are. Must be nice."

He smiled. "It's good to be a cat."

She rolled her neck and grinned. "Well, cat, our date with destiny awaits."

"Then let's go meet it."

CHAPTER TWENTY-SEVEN

Scarlett walked through the quiet warehouse and out the door on the far side. Lin joined her before she stepped through. Together, they went to where a ring of shielded Witches watched over the box a couple hundred feet away from the building.

Lin ordered, "Everyone else, get to a safe distance. We don't know what's gonna happen."

Scarlett touched her fingers to the hilts of her throwing knives. "It'll be fine." She wasn't sure who she was trying to convince.

Lin stepped beside her and muttered, "This is a bad idea." The drow's hand rested on the crossbow at her thigh. She was fully armed and armored as if she'd be joining the fight. It only made sense, but Scarlett had no intention of messing with the rules Camus had set.

"It's the only one we've got."

"Doesn't make it better."

The portal blossomed into existence and revealed only

darkness on the far side. Scarlett stated, "I'll go first in case it's a trap."

Lin countered, "We'll go together."

Runeclaw snapped, "Agreed."

She didn't argue. There was no point. The three walked abreast through the portal, from one night to another.

Camus smiled at the sight of the trio coming through the portal. He twitched his staff, and the torches around the plateau's perimeter sprang to fiery life, sending sparks into the sky to join the stars overhead.

The women froze and stared at him. It was almost impossible to believe the moment had arrived. He'd been at the plateau for hours, building energy and deepening his connection to the place. Now he was full to bursting with magical power.

So many years and so much blood had built up the magic in this place. The notion that the witch thought she might defeat him here, on his plateau, made him laugh with real pleasure. This was what he should feel like all the time. This was truly living. He was fully himself here like nowhere else.

He felt the eyes upon him, but no one spoke. He flicked a finger against his staff to dispatch the veil hiding his captives, who were still locked rigidly in place with force magic. "Your friend can step back through the portal, then pull them through. Move quickly. The portal will close soon."

The witch looked at her friend and nodded. The drow stepped back and tugged against his hold on his captives. He resisted for a moment out of spite, then let them go. As soon as they were through the portal, he dropped it.

He had to give the other woman credit. She drew and fired her crossbow in the second it took for the portal to disappear.

The world shifted into seeming slow motion as the bolt flew toward him. The magic he'd pumped into his reflexes, muscles, and senses took hold to give him the opportunity to react. He flicked a finger against his staff again, and a burst of shadow magic shot out and destroyed the bolt before it could reach him. The portal closed fully, and he turned his attention to the witch.

Scarlett spoke. "That wasn't my choice."

Camus, who she decided to call Red for short, replied, "It was expected. A valued friend would have to try."

She tensed as his hand went behind his back, but it only came out with a helmet he placed on his head. It was an ornate thing that appeared to be made of scales. She forced herself not to react as Runeclaw moved slowly off to her left toward a space where their foe couldn't attack both of them at once. "Is this the only option? I mean, we're not going out for coffee or anything, but you could live, even if your life is restricted in jail."

She tapped her wand and threaded magic into her muscles and senses as she spoke. The improvement opened her to the aura of the place, which was deeply unsettling. It was like something was rotting nearby, and she could only catch the scent of it now and again. When she did, the sense of wrongness was almost debilitating.

The man across the plateau from her laughed. "You truly believe you'll win and are offering me mercy?" He shook his head. "No, we will have it out here, once and for all."

Scarlett ignored whatever he said next and swept her gaze around the plateau. It was an empty, mostly flat space with its edges demarcated by the torches. She imagined a huge fall awaited beyond them. Above was sky and stars, nowhere she recognized. It would be a lousy place to die. Her mental voice kicked in. *Well, maybe you should focus, then.*

Camus raised his arms and relaxed the leash on his power. Slowly, at first evidenced only by a ripple in the torch flames, a wind began to form. It moved in a circle around the plateau's perimeter as it grew in intensity.

Debris flew into the air and bounced off the shields covering him, the witch, and the cat. It also knocked the witch back a half-step, and her look of surprise drew a smile from him. His power here was more than she expected. Well, it should be. This was his place. Home territory.

He increased the wind until it halted the cat's progress, and the witch fought against it. He laughed, turned his head to the sky, and shouted, "Come to me, my pets." The wind was only a defensive measure so his foes couldn't reach him. He felt the first stirring of his minions as the ground shuddered underfoot.

The woman and the cat attempted to move forward but failed against the strong wind. She threw lightning at him, but his shields handled it easily. The wind increased and the rumbling grew, as did his anticipation of the battle's true beginning, which was only seconds away.

Scarlett focused her magic and will to keep the wind at bay but couldn't do more than hold her place. A couple of dozen feet away from her, Runeclaw had a similar challenge. Doubts encroached on her mind. Red was stronger than she thought and more powerful than he'd revealed the previous times they mixed it up. She wondered if he had taken a potion that increased his magic potential before she arrived. She'd never heard of such a thing, but as she'd discovered again and again, there was a lot she didn't know.

She had planned to rush into hand-to-hand range and defeat him with fists, feet, and knives instead of getting into a protracted battle with magic because she'd judged his physical skills were less than hers. That option was no longer on the table.

Scarlett went with the other plan she'd made for the start of the fight, drew her pistol from the small of her back, and pulled the trigger once. She assumed he would have defenses to protect him from such a move, but that didn't mean it wasn't worth attempting in case he was stupid enough not to. That was also why she only tried one round.

The bullet passed through him. He looked down and brushed his shirt where it had struck.

She muttered, "Damn, illusion," and returned the gun to its holster. It was a logical choice, the same one she would've made in his place. She pushed her magical senses, but the place was so overwhelming she couldn't get any real sense of anything other than the oppressive sense of wrongness. Her frown deepened as he stood there after his shout, and she wondered what he was waiting for. She doubted she would enjoy finding out.

Scarlett threaded her magic toward Runeclaw, linked to his pendant, and connected to him through it. His greater senses shared through that channel gave her an idea of where Red was. Not too far distant from his illusion but far enough that a shot would miss.

She reached for a throwing knife, figuring a throw at his real location might be enough of a surprise to succeed, then froze as the ground under her feet trembled. Her head whipped around to check on Runeclaw as she bent her knees to avoid falling. He stared back with concern written on his face.

A moment later, pieces of earth exploded from the ground all across the plateau. Scarlett doubled the shields around her and Runeclaw to handle the debris that rained down. Larger forms fell alongside the rocks, dirt, and stone. *Humanoid* forms.

Her eyes widened as she stared at them. They were corpses in various states of disrepair, some mostly bones, others seeming as if they might've been buried moments before. The wands and staves some held radiated menace but weren't as overtly threatening as the way the rest flexed their hands to display the sharp claws they all shared. With a loud cry that came from every voice simultaneously, they charged.

CHAPTER TWENTY-EIGHT

Scarlett forced herself into motion as the wind continued to whip around in an effort to compromise her balance. She quickly sorted the enemies coming toward her into magical and non-magical threats, bolstered her shields, and decided to go for the latter first. It was unlikely the magicals would have the power to get through her shields, but she didn't know about those claws.

Anticipating that Red would intercept ranged magical attacks, she reached back and drew her long knives from her back sheaths. The first enemy to approach her was a skeleton clad in a few scraps of fabric. One blade chopped off its head while the other severed an arm.

It fell to pieces as she spun into her next blow, going low against a creature that was part skeleton and part flesh. The blade she whipped into its side got stuck, forcing her to drop it as the rotting corpse fell. She beheaded it with the other knife.

A front kick knocked the next one away from her, and she ran parallel to the line toward Runeclaw, who was darting around to evade the few enemies who had chosen to come at him. A blast of magic sizzled against her shield, and she snarled a curse as she drew her wand and turned toward the attacker.

He sent another blast of focused flame at her. She met it with frost that shattered upon impact, destroying her foe and peppering the nearby enemies with icy shrapnel. She grabbed one of the grenades from her belt, primed it, and tossed it into a group advancing toward her a short distance away. It detonated, taking out the non-magicals and momentarily distracting the magicals as they defended against the flying shrapnel.

She ran at her next foe, a man in tattered robes that might once have been a light blue. He threw magic at her feet in an attempt to trip her up. She jumped to avoid it and buried her knife in his sternum as she reached him.

His force shield held for a moment before her momentum and power pushing against his opened it enough for the blade to sink in. She rode him down to the ground, jumped off, and did a diving somersault in case someone attacked.

The wind struck and knocked her back toward the plateau's edge. She barely stopped herself before it threw her over the edge, then looked down and saw that yes, indeed, it was a *very* long drop. She jumped to her feet, shouted, "Stay away from the edges, buddy," and headed toward the next nearest threat.

Runeclaw had been evading blasts of magic from one of the new arrivals who had a pathological hatred of cats, to judge by his face. The creature moved with stuttering jerks that damaged his aim, fortunately for Runeclaw.

The cat pushed against the wind that tried to buffet him toward the edge. When it shifted, he made progress toward his enemy. The wind returned in full force after a few seconds, forcing him to fight to stay in place while dodging the magical attacks. He'd tried testing lightning on the man, but it hadn't made it through his opponent's shield.

He thought "man" probably wasn't an appropriate description for whatever this thing was now. A corpse animated by magic, probably. He didn't know if such a thing was possible, but he'd also seen ghosts in the Driskill Hotel, so he wasn't about to rule anything out.

The wind shifted again, and he darted toward his foe. The man smiled and raised his staff, timing his blow for when Runeclaw would arrive. Runeclaw feinted to the right, then drove between the man's legs. The staff smacked down an instant too late, spearing the earth behind him.

Runeclaw turned and leapt. His claws sank into the tattered black robes covering the man, and he used them to pull himself up. His enemy spun and caused the robes to flare out, but Runeclaw stayed locked on and continued climbing. With a snarl, the man barked a word and was suddenly covered in fire.

The cat jumped to the top of the man's bald head as the flames consumed the fabric. He raked his claws over the man's face, the sides of his head, and the back of his neck.

His opponent didn't react as he'd expected. There were

no screams, no gushing blood. Instead, the thing reached up, grabbed him, and tried to throw him. Runeclaw sank his claws into the thing's arm, and the moment he had the leverage, hurtled toward its face again.

He savaged its neck with his claws, ripping at it with all that was in him. The force shield around the man couldn't hold up against his sharp nails, and finally, after far too long, the damage reached a critical point. The being grabbed his throat and sank to the ground.

Runeclaw jumped off, wiped his bloody paws in the dirt, and looked for another opponent.

Camus scowled at the sight in front of him. The witch was handling his pets, which wasn't completely unexpected, but he'd assumed they could take care of the cat. He gathered more magic from the plateau, drinking in large gulps. He dispatched small amounts in focused strikes at the witch and her pet, but their shields failed to break. Still, he would continue to test them continuously and do what he could to drain their defensive energy while focusing on his next play.

He saw himself as if from outside, his awareness becoming one with the plateau's pulsing energy. So much blood and so many lives, all sunk into this patch of earth and waiting for his touch. He opened the channels wide to draw in as much as he could. The power pushed at the boundaries of his skin, and still he built it and harried his enemies. Still he waited to reach the point where he couldn't hold it back any longer.

Scarlett charged at the pair of wizards, one of whom had a wand and the other a staff. She'd brought one of her knives back to her hand and carried it and her wand. She stabbed at them, but they parted and spun out of the way, displaying impressive agility for corpses.

Dual blasts hit her simultaneously but failed to penetrate her shields. She was pleasantly surprised that her defenses were standing up as well as they were against the attacks of these creatures and the ones Red was throwing at her. It made her wonder if this was a distraction and if so, what she was being distracted from.

She whipped the long knife around in a wild swing designed to make one of the magicals backpedal, then blasted the other with force magic. It should have thrown him over the edge but only knocked him back a few feet. It was as if something in this place somehow blunted all of her direct magic.

Scarlett growled, "Fine, then," and threw the large knife at one of the pair. She used that hand to grab Fang and hurl the dagger after the knife. She controlled Fang's path with her wand and pushed with her magic to increase its speed. The dagger spun parallel to the ground as it flew forward and slashed the neck of one, then the other.

The dagger whipped around back to her hand as the two grabbed their throats and fell. She'd discovered that only throat strikes worked against them and had no idea why, not that it mattered. With no other enemies nearby, she turned, located Red, and started toward him.

Camus watched the witch advance with a smile. It was too late for her to intervene. If she'd cut through the chaff faster, she might have had a chance to stop him before he'd gathered all the power he needed. She hadn't.

He floated several feet into the air, then released his magic in a focused beam at the ground. When it struck, the earth convulsed and knocked the woman and the cat from their feet. Pieces of the ground broke apart and hovered in the air before clumping together.

Inch by inch, foot by foot, the earth built a colossal figure twenty feet high. It was humanoid with an oversized head, oversized feet, and oversized hands. Everything about it was huge and powerful. Its knuckles were boulders. Its sinews were roots and branches.

He sensed the blood of those who had died here pulsing inside it, filling all of it, creating red bubbles for eyes. The creation of this giant was the utmost secret left to him from the previous leaders of the Veil, a spell that had taken decades to perfect. He had worked hard to master the spell by creating smaller versions to test but had never invoked the full magic of the place as he did now.

His awareness split again. He felt himself as the plateau, the small floating creature, and the giant who bellowed at the puny witch and cat as they got to their feet. It was almost too much to take, and he felt his sanity cracking at the edges. The sensation made him laugh again. He was truly a being of power now, and whatever the cost, it was worth it.

Scarlett couldn't believe what she saw. She stood stunned, watching the creature grow layer by layer, bit by bit. A rational corner of her mind screamed for her to run, but she couldn't make her body move. She wasn't physically locked in place, but her mind refused to do anything except gape at what it saw. The creature's roar finally broke her out of her reverie.

She growled, "Oh, bloody hell. Runeclaw, go after Red. I'll deal with this thing."

CHAPTER TWENTY-NINE

Scarlett ran at the creature as it lumbered toward her. When it was still twenty feet or so away, she grabbed the remaining grenades on her belt and threw them at it, one after the other. The first landed at its foot and blew out a chunk. The second hit the other leg and removed more of the earth that made it up. The third went high, detonated at about stomach level, and accomplished very little.

She snarled a curse as Red blasted her with shadow magic and darted to her right to put the creature between them. As she dashed away, leading the monster toward the edge where she thought she might be able to knock it over, she pushed more magic into her body. It came sluggishly, probably because she'd already done this and must be near maximum capacity. Still, it was clear that this thing would take everything she had.

She cut to her left, and it sidestepped and swung a massive foot at her. The blow arrived surprisingly quickly for such a big thing, and Scarlett barely managed to throw up layers of force shields to prevent it from hitting her body. She slid, popped up, and kept running as it tried to stomp down on her. When she thought she'd gained enough distance, she stopped, spun, and drew a throwing knife. She hurled it at the creature with the random hope it might accomplish something.

The giant swatted it out of the air with a deep rumble that sounded like laughter, then dropped to its knees and pounded both fists onto the ground in front of her. The blow sent her sprawling backward and knocked her wand out of her hand.

Runeclaw tried to ignore the huge beast prowling around the other part of the plateau. His fundamental instincts pushed him to help Scarlett, but despite the fact that size disparities normally didn't bother him in fights, that thing had to be an exception. Hopefully it would go down when he took care of the wizard.

Red was distracted during Runeclaw's initial prowl in his direction, but then his gaze cut over. Runeclaw froze as the earth before him exploded as it had when the first creatures appeared. Nothing emerged from the ground, and his instincts propelled him forward in a mad dash.

The ground continued to explode around him, one spot after the next, as if he were running through a minefield. He wove left and right, stopped and started unpredictably, and did his best to avoid the flying debris. A sudden roar behind him caused him to skid to a stop and spin. A smaller version of the giant had appeared, one as proportionally large to his stature as the one Scarlett faced. He muttered, "Oh, hell," and steeled himself for battle.

He dashed away at an angle that would allow him to keep the monster and the wizard in view so he could act if an opportunity presented itself. The perspective included Scarlett's giant. While his was slower and no doubt weaker than that one, it still seemed formidable enough. On the positive side, any energy the wizard expended on him was power he wasn't sending against Scarlett.

He didn't know how to defeat the thing, but that didn't matter. He'd have to go through it to get to the wizard because he couldn't leave it at his back, so he would. He rushed forward as the other creature raced toward him. Runeclaw ignored the blast of lightning that struck the earth behind him. Soon, he would have the creature between himself and the wizard again and wouldn't have to worry about that.

Unexpectedly, the creature threw itself into the air in an attempt to tackle Runeclaw. He skidded to a stop and scampered to the side but still received a glancing blow from the thing's fist. He tumbled to the side, snarled, and shot it with electricity. The attack accomplished exactly nothing. Runeclaw angrily climbed to his feet and charged after it again.

Camus looked through the eyes of the giant chasing the witch and felt its limbs as if they were his. His body continued to float a few feet off the ground, wrapped in protective shields. He kept one eye on the cat's battle as he immersed the rest of himself into the pleasure of controlling the giant.

The earth trembled with every footfall as he ran after the witch, who had regained her feet and weapons. She threw a knife at him again, and he batted it to the side. She stopped, set herself, and hit him with a force blast that had to use much of her power.

It blew out a chunk of his shoulder but managed nothing else. The surrounding earth filled the gap, making him a little smaller and that arm a little lower, but it still worked. He demonstrated that by charging forward and delivering an open-hand strike that encompassed her entire body. She flew thirty feet across the plateau before bouncing on the ground and losing her wand and the knife she'd had in the other hand.

He laughed as he stomped after her in pursuit. He would smash her until there was only a hint of life left in her, then he would kick her off the mountain for good measure. Afterward, he'd do the same to the cat. He didn't need their blood added to his plateau. He would erase them from the world and his memory, and that would be for the best.

Only a few moments more, and this farce with the witch would be over for good.

Runeclaw scrambled away from the thing as it pounded on the earth. He couldn't see how he was going to get rid of it. Each time he dashed in to claw, it took the blow and returned one that he was hard-pressed to avoid. He sent a mental message to Scarlett. *Can you make me stronger?*

She didn't reply, but he felt magic flow through the channel that connected them. He became faster and felt stronger. His size didn't change, but he had more to work with inside. He'd considered himself pretty much optimal but had been incorrect. That had promise for future battles, assuming he survived this one.

The next time the creature hit him, it only knocked him back a few feet rather than sending him tumbling. Runeclaw grinned. Now he had something to work with.

He stalked toward the creature, then stumbled to the side to tempt it into an attack. It lifted both hands high and slammed them down as he jumped to the side. Runeclaw ran between the creature's legs, spun, and savaged the back of its leg where its calf met its heel.

He sliced at the spot repeatedly, chopping shards of earth away. When the thing turned to counter, he turned with it and continued savaging that spot. It attempted to kick him, but he dodged, and when the foot came back down, he continued to attack that spot. Finally, a slash severed the link between leg and foot. Its foot transformed into earth, disconnected from the rest, and dropped. The creature fell to the side, its balance compromised.

A foot began to reappear, but he'd accomplished what he needed to do by bringing it to the ground. Runeclaw dashed forward and clawed its throat, the same place that had worked for the zombies. It frantically batted at him with its massive hands, but his magically enhanced speed allowed him to dodge out of the way each time. When he'd created a hole in its throat, he shoved his tail into it and slammed all the magic he held into a lightning blast.

The thing stiffened for an instant, glowed, and exploded into pieces, showering the area with earth and blood and sending Runeclaw flying. He landed on his feet, spat out some of the spray that had gotten in his mouth, growled, "Gross," and ran toward the floating wizard.

Scarlett wiped dirt off her face as she scrambled out of the way of the onrushing giant. She'd been sloppy and had gotten slapped for her trouble. Her shields had held, but she couldn't be sure they would do so a second time.

As she ran, she pulled her backup wand from her boot and brought her main wand and Fang back to her hands. She shoved her backup wand in her belt, sheathed Fang, and grabbed the potions on her belt as she continued to flee. She quaffed a healing potion to counteract her growing headache and an energy potion to hopefully give her enough power to defeat the creature.

When her mind cleared, she made a plan. Runeclaw had communicated that electricity worked from the inside, and she had only one idea of how to make that happen. She skidded to a stop at the plateau's edge and turned. The giant rumbled toward her with a smug look that had to be the wizard controlling it.

Scarlett ran at it, jogging at first, then used magic to make herself faster and to supplement her jump as she leapt with a loud cry. Time slowed as she arced toward the giant with her wand in her left hand and Fang in her right.

She could picture where the blade would sink into the thing's eye. When it did, she'd shove her wand in beside it and trigger the strongest electrical blast she could manage. Hopefully the thing would detonate from the inside like Runeclaw's had.

Then she'd land, spin, and hurl Fang at him while the wizard was reeling from the feedback of his spell being destroyed. Hopefully, the blade would have enough poison left that even a scratch would work. She considered asking Fang if it did, but all her thoughts were driven from her head as a hand, moving impossibly fast, intercepted her flight and smashed her down into the ground.

Scarlett tasted blood as everything around her swirled into darkness.

CHAPTER THIRTY

Pain and awareness came back to Scarlett in tandem. She had no idea how long she'd been out. Her entire body throbbed with the brutal impact despite the shields that protected her lessening it.

The most disconcerting thing was the burning in the center of her chest. Her first thoughts were that she'd broken her ribs, then that her heart was torn. She finally got enough brainpower together to focus on it and realized it was her grandmother's pendant, hot as flame against her skin. The pain lasted only a moment in that location, then shot through her entire body from toes to fingers to scalp.

The pain was brief. When it vanished, power filled the space it left behind. It was power with that same rancid aura she'd detected before, but it was still something she could use. It filled her to bursting with energy.

Scarlett threw herself to the side and into a roll to avoid whatever attack would come next, just in time to avoid a foot stomp that made the ground tremble behind her. She continued her roll, then angled herself into the air with a burst of force magic to land on her feet.

She'd lost Fang but pointed her wand toward where it had been and snapped the summoning charm. The dagger flew into her hand. She growled, "All right, then. Let's try this again, you bastard."

The thing ran toward her with a rage-filled bellow. She screamed her anger as she charged toward it. Flicks of magic created force barriers in layers around her, spreading out and out and out. She jumped again when the moment felt right, aiming for its eye. It lowered its head as it clapped its hands toward her, but she used a quick burst of force magic to adjust her path and the hands were a moment too late.

She hit its face, and Fang sank into its eye as intended. The hands had hit her force shields but failed to stop her. She touched her wand to the dagger and channeled all her newfound energy and power into it. It was too much for the creature. It exploded and sent her flying across the plateau. She whipped out a band of force and grabbed onto a boulder to halt her flight before she was over the edge, then landed.

Runeclaw ran over to her. "Nice job."

"Nice job, you. You're the one who came up with the solution."

"Well, I am the smart one in our relationship."

Scarlett laughed, still feeling tipsy from the power she'd channeled. "Okay, genius. Let's go end this, shall we?"

Camus gaped, stunned. When the witch destroyed his creature, he fell a few feet to the ground. The impact had shocked him back into his mind. He lost his wider sense of the plateau along with his sense of connection to the giant. The power of the place was still there, but it seemed reduced and farther away.

With a snarl, he rose and ripped off his crimson robes to reveal the armor underneath. He leveled his staff and blasted force and fire through it, first aimed at the witch, then at the cat. The flames should've obliterated them both, fueled as they were by the plateau's power. When he finished, they were still standing, unharmed. He sputtered, "How?"

The witch shook her head with a laugh. "I have no idea. If I had to bet, the universe doesn't want a scumbag like you to win."

She charged toward him, and he attempted to blast her with every form of magic he knew. The assaults struck her shield and slid away without doing damage. He gritted his teeth. "Fine, we'll do it the hard way." He set his feet and readied his staff to smash the woman when she got close enough.

Scarlett reached him and feinted with Fang, then whipped her wand around. She'd covered it in force magic and extended it to be more like a fighting stick. She landed blows on his armor with both of them, but the strange metal scales turned the attacks with ease. He used his staff to counter with a straight vertical strike at her head, and she had to whip her weapons back and across to deflect it.

His strength was prodigious, fueled by the magic of this place. While she still possessed some of it, her body could only hold so much power. He was naturally larger and stronger than her, which meant he'd eventually win if she allowed him to strike like that.

Scarlett disengaged with a twirl and backed away. Runeclaw whispered in her mind, *Hide me*. She spun in another circle and flicked her wand to cast a veil over the cat while her back was to Red.

She faced him in time to bash his staff away with her wand and Fang. She feinted at the small bit of flesh around his mouth that the helmet didn't cover and nicked his lip. He reached up, dabbed at the blood, then looked at it. "You'll pay for that, witch."

Since he didn't immediately fall over from the tranquilizing poison, she figured it must've been spent. She steeled herself. "Bring it on, scalehead."

Runeclaw stalked behind the wizard, knowing he would have only one shot to intervene in the battle. Scarlett increased the ferocity of her attacks, throwing in magic to keep the wizard's attention on her. They circled as they fought, requiring Runeclaw to pause at times and redirect at others. Throughout his approach, he kept his eyes locked on the wizard, searching for any vulnerability.

Eventually, he saw one. Flashes of skin showed where the helmet didn't quite meet the armor when Red turned his head a certain way. It was small, almost so tiny as to be illusory. Still, it was there, and it was an opportunity he needed to take.

He continued closing as they fought. Then, recognizing what Scarlett was about to do from the times he'd watched her spar with other people, he leapt toward the wizard.

Her attack came in toward Red's midsection, which caused him to bend forward as he blocked down. That opened the gap at the back of his neck. Runeclaw's leap took him to the man's shoulders, and he raked his claws along the back of the wizard's neck, cutting through the shield and deep into the flesh.

Red screamed and jerked back. One hand left the staff to bat at the back of his neck.

Scarlet had sensed Runeclaw's approach and worked to move Red into a position that might give the cat an opportunity. It had worked. She rushed forward, drew Fang back, and with all the physical and magical strength she possessed, stabbed the man's shoulder. His face blanched as he dropped the staff, grabbed the dagger's hilt, and crumpled.

He reached for the potions on his belt, but she used her wand to flick them away before he could grab them. She smiled. "When you're unconscious, we'll take you to a nice place where you can think about your actions, well, forever."

He moaned but didn't otherwise respond. Blood

trickled out from under his fingers where they pressed on his shoulder and made trails down his armor.

Runeclaw jumped to her shoulder and looked down at the figure. "You didn't kill him."

She shook her head. "No. I thought he should have some time to think about what he's done. Then maybe we give all the people he captured an opportunity to beat him with a roll of coins in a sock."

Runeclaw laughed. "Evil. I like it."

A tremor from below caught her attention. Blood dripped onto the ground from Red's wound, and suddenly the earth trembled again.

She backed up, and moments later the earth erupted. Large swaths of dirt and roots rose over the wizard, dropped on top of him, and retreated. When they were gone, so was he. No sign of him remained, nor did any indication that the plateau had been disrupted. She looked at Runeclaw.

The cat observed, "Lame."

The comment made her laugh. "Yeah. But you know, I think this might turn out to be a worse result for him. Could be that someday he'll come back as a lackey for some other Veil wizard."

Runeclaw replied, "Well, if so, we'll just have to beat him again."

"Well said, my friend."

"Well done, Guardian."

CHAPTER THIRTY-ONE

The next morning, Scarlett was in Wheels early as she'd been so many times before. The place was mostly refinished, and the cleaning crew was doing its work around her. Most importantly, the mugs had returned to join the coffee urn, and she had a steaming cup of hot coffee beside her.

Her mind was curiously free of worry. It seemed like forever since she'd been this calm and relaxed. Runeclaw was laid out on his side on the table, getting a little extra sleep. He hadn't been particularly excited when she woke him to come to Wheels, but since this was her last day in town—her last hours, actually—she wanted to soak in as much as she could.

Maddox and Snow entered the front door together and headed for the coffee. Once they had mugs, they sat at her table. Maddox prompted, "All right, the whole story, right now. Wren said it's a good one."

Scarlett laughed. She'd told Lin and Wren the tale the night before. She related her experiences from the message onward to the Spell Riders and provided all the gory details about the fight on the plateau.

When she finished, Runeclaw interjected, "It was all me, really."

Everyone laughed, and Scarlett replied, "It always is."

They chatted for a while longer. Then it was finally time. Wren came over and hugged Scarlett. "You're always welcome here. We know you can portal, so don't you dare be a stranger."

Maddox and Snow hugged her in turn, and the latter added, "Same here. Regular visits."

Scarlett drew a cross over her heart with a finger. "I promise. My explorations will be punctuated with frequent stops home to see my family."

From his spot on her shoulder, Runeclaw added, "Don't worry. If she forgets, I'll claw her until she remembers."

Scarlett made the rounds of the room to say goodbye to the other people she knew. She lingered with Amber. "You know, you could still come with us."

The infomancer grinned. "My work isn't exactly mobile. Besides, I can be in your ear anytime you want. Wear your glasses so I can see what you're doing."

"You know it." They embraced, and Scarlett headed outside. Lin's motorcycle was parked beside Dusk Runner, and the drow was cinching up her bulging saddlebags. Scarlett's were also packed full with her normal stuff plus camping gear and road snacks. They'd portal when they needed to but wanted to be mostly self-sufficient or as much as was reasonable.

Scarlett activated the bike's enchantments and created the force band for Runeclaw. He jumped up. "Where to?"

She threw a leg over the bike's saddle and settled in. "The Grand Canyon, like I said. Maybe we'll go from there to Yellowstone."

He turned to look at her and said with suspicion, "Uh-huh."

"I'm sure there will be other enjoyable stuff along the way, plus camping on the open road. It'll be fun. You'll see."

The suspicion had not left his tone. "All right."

Lin had climbed onto her motorcycle. "You should tell him."

Scarlett countered, "You should shut up."

The cat was already out of the bag, so to speak. Runeclaw demanded, "Tell me what?"

Scarlett sighed. "All right, there is a potato museum on the way. And a ghost town." She couldn't hide her excitement about the latter.

He turned away from her and dug his claws into the force band. "I hate you."

She patted his head. "You love me."

Lin called, "Next up, Grand Canyon," and pulled onto the road. Scarlett followed, then pulled up to ride beside her friend. She stared at the horizon and realized she was as happy as she'd ever been. She didn't know what her future would bring but was positive it would be full of adventures, laughs, and all the annoyance a supremely snarky cat could bring.

AUTHOR NOTES: TR CAMERON

AUGUST 31, 2024

Another series wrapped! I hope you enjoyed where it went, and where it wound up. There's a thing in writing called the rule of threes (well, that rule's everywhere, I guess), and subconsciously everyone should have been waiting for a third visit to the plateau. I hope the payoff was as fun to read as it was to write!

I'm now in that reset period where my brain starts bubbling with new ideas for the next series. I've got the broad strokes figured out, but the details are where the good stuff lives, and those are still a little murky. It will be tonally similar to my first Oriceran series, *Federal Agents of Magic*, in that it will be very much a team-based ensemble cast. But the subject matter is quite different. The first book, Codename: Rockstar, has Spellbound Security protecting an international superstar from those who wish them harm. It's going to be fun!

I recently attended the Killer Nashville author conference in Franklin, TN. It's thriller and crime focused, but my work incorporates a number of those themes. I learned some useful things, though not enough for me personally to justify the cost of going back again anytime soon. Then I caught a bug and spent the last days of the conference and most of the next week in bed recovering. During that time, I rewatched several movies (Clear and Present Danger, meh, Sum of All Fears, good, and Atomic Blonde, great) and the first season of Altered Carbon. I'd forgotten how much I liked that show. I had read at least one of the books before it became a series and was already a fan, but the style and storytelling of the show is impressive.

I attended the Midwest Writing Workshop in Muncie, IN. It was a nice getaway from my normal life and a chance to be in the author headspace exclusively for a few days. I enjoyed the experience. The panels weren't right for me, though, which happens. I don't think I'll be back, but I would encourage anyone interested in authorness who's nearby to check it out. Really looking forward to Killer Nashville next month.

September's chaos has been added to. We're seeing Green Day a second time the day after our Pittsburgh show, and there's a possible addition of In This Moment / Avatar / Tek2, who we saw in Buffalo with Ice Nine Kills. That's in addition to all the other stuff. I'll be posting some travel stuff on Facebook probably. I'm in logistical planning for our trip to Vegas for When We Were Young in October, which involves lots of internet searching on how to survive it when you're old. The answer seems to be back support, really good shoes, and Liquid IV. It's daunting. But it's got the potential to be a really good core memory for me and the kid both if I can pull it off.

Hozier was amazing. I'm not a huge fan or anything,

but the night was gorgeous despite the tornado warnings before hand, the opener was good, and Hozier had eight musicians on stage with him. It was a luxurious sort of sound, with gorgeous visuals. Very glad we went. We paid for fancy, but not the fanciest, parking, and that was nice too. I was going to pay for the fanciest parking for Avril Lavigne, but it turned out to be way more expensive than expected, so no, not doing that. Going to be a rough week of trying to learn Avril's setlist and Weezer's for the second of our two-nights-two-shows in September.

I find *The Boys* to be the weirdest show ever. It's so painfully awkward to watch that I usually make it partway through the first episode and then walk away for months. That's happened again. The kid and I are continuing to watch Jodie Whittaker's *Doctor Who*, now in Season 13. The stakes are really ratcheted up right at the start, and I'm interested to see where it goes, and how it gets from there to the return of David Tennant.

We saw *Deadpool & Wolverine* twice and I just have to say... so wrong, but so good. The threads woven into it from the larger MCU are brilliant. The gag with the most important Cameo was so amazing as to be unprecedented and showed such knowledge (and love) of the Marvel Universe. I could have done without some of the Wade-as-normal-dude scenes, but that's been a part of all the films. And the fourth wall breaks were fantastic. It was great to get to share it with the kid, who had been resistant to watching the Deadpool films before the third one came out. I'm rooting for a Channing Tatum *Gambit* film now.

American Gods, as expected, has grabbed me in Audio. The narrator is great, and the person who does Mr.

Wednesday sounds so much like Ian McShane, who played the character on the screen, that I had to look it up to see if it was him. I'm alternating that with the Jack Ryan books by Tom Clancy. I'm a sucker for geopolitical intrigue, apparently. On the page, I've started the new James S.A. Corey novel. It couldn't be less like *The Expanse*, which is a good thing I suppose, although it makes me want to reread those books and rewatch the series. My kid's not quite ready for that level of sci-fi, I think.

Normally September is when I go back to teaching after summer break, but for the first time in my life I'm experiencing that ultimate perk of academia, the sabbatical. It's very, very weird and somewhat humbling to see that everything continues on quite well in my absence. But if I don't get to work on the course development project I'm supposed to be doing, I'm going to be in trouble. So that deadline pressure, at least, is unchanged!

Thanks again for joining me for *The Nomad Witch*. I hope you'll come along for *Spellbound Security*!

Until next month, joys upon joys to you.

Standard monthly reminders - If you're not part of the Oriceran Fans Facebook group, **join**! There's a pizza giveaway every month, and Martha and (usually) I and all sort of fun author folks show up via Zoom to chat with our readers. It's a great time, and the community feel to it is truly fantastic. The group is very welcoming and enthusiastic. Oriceran Fans. Facebook. Your phone is probably within reach. Do it!

Before I go, if this series is your first taste of my Urban

Fantasy, look for "Magic Ops." I promise you'll enjoy it, and you'll like Diana, Rath, and company. You might also enjoy my science fiction work. All my writing is filled with action, snark, and villains who think they're heroes. Drop by www.trcameron.com and take a look!

Your monthly reminder that you can find the free prequel short story for The Nomad Witch series, "Vacation Day," here: https://dl.bookfunnel.com/rxccsvm5jn

PS: If you'd like to chat with me, here's the place. I check in daily or more: https://www.facebook.com/AuthorTRCameron. Often, I put up interesting and/or silly content there, as well. For more info on my books, and to join my reader's group, please visit www.trcameron.com.

AUTHOR NOTES: MARTHA CARR

SEPTEMBER 18, 2024

You know that little voice in your head? The one that says you should've done better, should've worked harder, or—heaven forbid—should've gotten out of bed before noon on Saturday? Yeah, that voice. Let's call it the Inner Critic, and it's time we have a serious talking to.

I know mine's bad when I'm in the shower and realize I'm answering back.

Here's the thing: We live in a bubble that's constantly telling us to do more, be more, achieve more. It's like there's a never-ending race and we're all expected to be Olympic-level competitors—at daily living. And let me tell you, I'm kind of tired. Tired of constantly falling short of some invisible, impossible standard that I set up and then acted like it was a new golden rule.

Take a moment and think about the last time you told yourself, "Wow, I'm really proud of how I handled that." It happens, but not often enough and more often for other people like we're in a special category.

Now, think about the last time you beat yourself up for

something, even something small. A late email reply? Forgetting to run an errand? That awkward thing you said in a meeting three years ago that still haunts you at 2 a.m.? That quick stop at QT for pizza. That one might be a Texas thing.

We're all pros at self-criticism, and not so great at self-kindness. It's in the same family of being sure something bad is about to happen, but can't believe the project we've worked so hard on will succeed.

There are probably a few reasons. Mine is the critical parents I got who saw everything that went wrong and let me know about it. And I don't think they invented that delightful practice. I'm sure they got an earful too. It's a learned behavior, which is good news. It means I can unlearn it.

Step one, I had to notice how often I turned away a compliment, or berated myself or stayed quiet in a conversation trying to fade away.

Step two, I made a decision to let go of that view of myself and just not care and start dancing like crazy, saying what I really meant and saying hello first. It's like its own magic trick.

Here's a better place to start to notice something we want to change. What would happen if we treated ourselves the way we treat our friends? What if, instead of beating ourselves up for missing the gym, we said, "Hey, you're doing your best. It's okay to rest." Or if we stopped feeling guilty for taking a day off, and instead recognized that sitting still is actually doing something worthwhile.

And here's where it gets interesting. When we start to be kinder to ourselves, something amazing happens: We actually become *more* productive. It's true! Studies show that people who practice self-compassion are more resilient, less stressed, and better able to tackle challenges. When we give ourselves a break, we stop wasting energy on guilt and shame, and we free up mental space for the things that really matter.

When I really stopped, with the help of a lot of friends, and a fair share of therapy, I was shocked at the amount of time that opened up for me. It's kind of like saying, I don't eat that much and then writing every bite down. It's always a shocker.

The next time that inner voice that actually has your best interests at heart, even though it doesn't sound like it, points out something. Say thank you and invite it to notice something worth celebrating about you. More adventures to follow.

It's time we all start giving ourselves the same kindness we so freely give to others. Because at the end of the day, life isn't about how much you get done, or how perfect you are. It's about showing up, trying your best, and giving yourself permission to take a break every now and then.

And if that break happens to involve a Netflix marathon and some ice cream, well, I'd say you've earned it.

OTHER SERIES FROM T.R. CAMERON

Urban Fantasy
(with Martha Carr and Michael Anderle)

Federal Agents of Magic (8 book series)
Scions of Magic (8 book series)
Magic City Chronicles (8 book series)
Rogue Agents of Magic (8 book series)
Witch Warrior (12 book series)
Secret Agent Witch (8 book series)

Science Fiction
(with Martha Carr and Michael Anderle)

Azophi Academy (4 book series)

OTHER SERIES IN THE ORICERAN UNIVERSE:

THE LEIRA CHRONICLES
CASE FILES OF AN URBAN WITCH
THE EVERMORES CHRONICLES
SOUL STONE MAGE
THE KACY CHRONICLES
MIDWEST MAGIC CHRONICLES
THE FAIRHAVEN CHRONICLES
I FEAR NO EVIL
THE DANIEL CODEX SERIES
SCHOOL OF NECESSARY MAGIC
SCHOOL OF NECESSARY MAGIC: RAINE CAMPBELL
ALISON BROWNSTONE
FEDERAL AGENTS OF MAGIC
SCIONS OF MAGIC
THE UNBELIEVABLE MR. BROWNSTONE
DWARF BOUNTY HUNTER
ACADEMY OF NECESSARY MAGIC
MAGIC CITY CHRONICLES
ROGUE AGENTS OF MAGIC

OTHER SERIES IN THE ORICERAN UNIVERSE:

OTHER BOOKS BY JUDITH BERENS

OTHER BOOKS BY MARTHA CARR

JOIN THE ORICERAN UNIVERSE FAN GROUP ON FACEBOOK!

CONNECT WITH THE AUTHORS

TR Cameron Social

Website: www.trcameron.com

Facebook: https://www.facebook.com/AuthorTRCameron

Martha Carr Social

Website: http://www.marthacarr.com

Facebook: https://www.facebook.com/groups/MarthaCarrFans/

Michael Anderle Social

Website: http://lmbpn.com

Email List: https://michael.beehiiv.com/

https://www.facebook.com/LMBPNPublishing

https://twitter.com/MichaelAnderle

https://www.instagram.com/lmbpn_publishing/

https://www.bookbub.com/authors/michael-anderle

BOOKS BY MICHAEL ANDERLE

Sign up for the LMBPN email list to be notified of new releases and special deals!

https://lmbpn.com/email/

For a complete list of books by Michael Anderle, please visit:

www.lmbpn.com/ma-books/

www.ingramcontent.com/pod-product-compliance
Lightning Source LLC
LaVergne TN
LVHW041801060526
838201LV00046B/1083